THEY
ALL
RAN
AWAY

THEY ALL RAN AWAY

EDWARD RONNS

WILDSIDE PRESS

THEY ALL RAN AWAY

1

BARNEY FORBES had been dreaming of Lily when he
awoke knowing that someone had quietly entered his
room. He did not move. He did not open his eyes. He
heard the sound of the mountain wind in the screens,
and he smelled the pines beyond the hotel window.

Someone breathed with heavy, laborious regularity,
not too far from his bed.

His dream of Lily faded, like the diminishing echoes
of a sorrowful song. Even while he listened to the other's
breathing, he thought, *It's getting better. It's over a year
now, and at last it's getting better.* There was a time
when he had awakened in a cold sweat, shouting her
name. There were other times when he had reached out
for her, had felt the emptiness of the bed beside him and
known she would never be there again, and those were
the worst times.

He let her fade out of his mind, and listened.

He heard the snap of the catches being opened on his
luggage, the rustle of his shirts being turned over, the
muted rattle of paper, the creak of a leather belt. And
the heavy breathing.

Barney opened his eyes to darkness.

A dim shape loomed over the luggage rack to his
right, a pencil torch an island of glowing light in an
invisible hand.

He had made no secret of his arrival in Omega, here
in the far Adirondacks. No secret about his intentions,

either. To hell with the old man's timid warnings. If you know there's a snake somewhere under the rocks, you start kicking the rocks around. If all the doors are closed against you, you have to start hammering on them. If you're looking for a dead man, you have to cry murder.

The only train available from New York had dropped him in Omega at eleven o'clock at night. His reservation at the resort hotel overlooking the lake was honored, somewhat to his surprise. But when he went to the police station at midnight, the sergeant's face froze; Barney all but heard that first door slam against him. At the Hunter estate, the big iron gates were not even opened. It did not bother him. He called it quits and turned in.

Now he judged by moonlight coming through the tall windows that it was about two o'clock in the morning. The man searching his luggage had his back to him. Quietly, silently, Barney moved his hand up from his side and under the pillow, seeking his gun.

His fingers touched the butt of the .38 Special—and then he froze as the intruder straightened up with a soft grunt. He was a big man, with slightly bowed shoulders, gray hair that looked silvery in the moonlight. The wind whined in the screens. There was a faint lapping sound of water from the lake shore. The pine trees thrashed. It was August, but here in the mountains the air was cold.

He closed his hand around the gun.

The intruder had ears like a cat—and a calm voice. "Take it easy, Mr. Forbes."

Barney sat up, the gun in his hand. "Don't mind me. Just tell me what you're looking for."

"Nothing special," the man said easily. "I'd know it if I found it."

"Who are you?" Barney asked.

"Cops."

"The hell you say. Sit down over there. Fold your hands on the back of your neck. Don't move too fast."

Barney heard the sound of heavy breathing. The pencil flash snicked out. The intruder didn't like his orders. In the dim moonlight, his face was a graven mask, blank, the eyes darkly studying him. The moonlight ran a liquid finger along the barrel of the gun in Barney's hand. The wind rattled the screens again. A lone cricket began to chirp out on the hotel lawn, making a cold and forlorn sound.

"You're mighty touchy," the big man said.

"And you're wide open," Barney said. "Cop or no cop. You picked the lock or used a key, it doesn't matter. It adds up to breaking and entering. How would you like a slug in your belly?"

"I wouldn't like that at all."

"Then sit down."

The man sat.

Barney reached out with his left hand and turned on a lamp. The Omega Hotel had no use for modern decor or streamlined frills. Its rooms were barren caverns furnished with the original heavy walnut of the General Grant era. The rocking-chair brigade that habitually took possession of the veranda facing the lake never objected. Some of them, from Barney's brief glimpse in the lobby, probably had started summering here along with General Grant.

"All right," Barney said. "Talk about it."

"You're Barney Forbes?"

"That's why you were rifling my bag, wasn't it?"

"I reckon."

"You said you're a cop."

"Chief Jacobus Hendrycks. You'll find a lot of Hudson Valley Dutch around here. Put down the gun. I got a wife and eight kids."

Barney sat on the edge of the big bed. He was a tall man, not quite thirty. He had thick dark hair, dark blue eyes that seemed black when he was angry, a competent nose and mouth. He was quietly and completely his own man. It was expressed in the way he carried himself, in everything he did.

Chief Hendrycks was also a tall man, but he had gone to fat around the edges, and not even the piney mountain air could help his asthma. His face was long, sad, and a little frightened. The fear showed in the slow flicker of his pale eyes, in the tight corners of his mouth, in the way he breathed. But Barney knew that this man was not afraid of him. The chief's fear was a general thing, perhaps habitual, something that was much bigger than any one man or the town itself.

"What's so important about me that you break into my room and check my luggage?" Barney asked.

"You're looking for Malcolm Hunter, aren't you?"

"I'm here to find him."

Hendrycks spread his hands, as if no further answer was necessary. "Well, then."

Barney was annoyed. "You don't think I'll find him?"

"Better pray you don't, son." The chief smiled sadly. "You wouldn't want to tangle with Malcolm Hunter, right or wrong, working for him or against him."

"He's as mean as that?"

"He runs things."

"Does he run you?" Barney asked quietly.

Hendrycks thought about it. He was in no hurry. He wore an old Army surplus canvas jacket against the cold bite of the mountain wind. Under that was a faded flannel shirt that could never stand another washing. His shoes were heavy, serviceable, dusty.

"That isn't a nice thing to suggest, Mr. Forbes. In a way, everybody in Omega gets pushed around a bit by the Hunters. They've been here a long time. They own the most land, own the bank, the newspaper, this here hotel. Malcolm Hunter likes to own things. That's the way it is." He paused, sighed. "I reckon you could say he owns a small piece of me, too."

Barney said: "You haven't shown me any tin yet."

"Oversight. You rushed things." Hendrycks pulled a wallet from his pocket, a battered badge. He wore a holstered Smith & Wesson under the canvas jacket. His hands were surprising, long and strong and fine. He smiled. "It ain't often the chief of police gets the tables turned on him like this. Like to be my own fault. You look over the credentials, Mr. Forbes. Then we'll get down to business and I'll ask a few questions of my own."

Barney returned the wallet. "What do you want to know?"

"Who hired you. Why you're here. What you think you're going to get done in Omega. And when you plan to take the train home."

"Would you like it if I just packed up now?"

"Tomorrow morning will do," Hendrycks said calmly.

"I'll put it as simply as I can," Barney told him. "I've been retained by the law firm of Peterman, Klassen, Smith, Woolley and Smith, of 98 Wall Street. I have a law office of my own in the same building, but nobody seems to know it. It's a closet. Peterman, and so forth, handle nothing but gilt-edged trusts and estates. They don't consider me quite respectable. I suspect they hired me because they didn't know what else to do, and didn't want to use anyone who might bring them publicity. They hate publicity like the Omega Chamber of Commerce would hate snow in August. They retained me because I used to be a detective, second grade, on the metropolitan police force, because I was an MP in the Army, because I was starving and willing to forget about my law practice for a time."

"Go on."

"One of their clients is Jan Stuyvesant Hunter. Do you know him?"

"Malcolm's older brother. Much older."

"Like a beaten-up eagle."

"That fits," Hendrycks nodded.

"Jan Hunter said his brother Malcolm had disappeared under what he chose to call a cloud. Last week. A certain guide and trapper here in Omega, one Alex Kane, also disappeared at the same time. Alex Kane's wife has been screaming that Malcolm killed her husband and ran. The fight, she says, was over her own sweet self. Well, I'm supposed to find Malcolm Hunter and if he's in trouble, I'm supposed to help him."

"He'll be found when he wants to be found. And he won't appreciate your help."

"I'll do what I'm paid for," Barney said. "Have I got the story straight?"

"Mostly." Hendrycks sighed again. "Are you a married man, Mr. Forbes?"

"I was."

Hendrycks looked alert. "Divorced?"

"My wife was killed in an auto accident two months after we were married," Barney said. "Is it important to you?"

"I'm sorry, son. I was just thinking of Mrs. Hunter."

"What about her?"

"You'll know it when you see it." Hendrycks stood up. His face was tired, gaunt, seamed. His hair looked white under the harsh light, like week-old snow on a city street. "I'll see you at the station tomorrow morning."

"Are you ordering me out of town?"

"You know I can't do that. I'm just advising it."

"Thanks. But I'm not going," Barney said. "Do you know where I can find Malcolm Hunter?"

"If I knew where Hunter was, I'd keep it to myself."

"I hoped you might help me," Barney said.

Hendrycks paused at the door. "I've given you the best advice I can. Go back to your closet on Wall Street, son. Forget about Malcolm Hunter."

"You make him sound dangerous."

"He is."

"Did he really chase after this trapper's wife?"

"I wouldn't know. He has the idea he's got the right to chase any woman in Omega. Like one of them lords of the Middle Ages."

"Do you think he killed Alex Kane, as Kane's wife says?"

Hendrycks shrugged. He looked defeated. "We don't have the body. Alex could be in the woods, hunting, or on a guide trip. He didn't necessarily have to tell Ferne where he was going."

"Ferne is Alex Kane's wife?"

"Right."

"Pretty?"

"Sexy."

"Have you looked for either Kane or Hunter?"

"Better ask Straehle about that. He's the D.A."

"Straehle put the clamps on you?"

Hendrycks shrugged again. "Take that train in the morning, son. You won't get anywhere in Omega."

He started out. Barney said: "One thing, chief. What were you looking for in my bags?"

Hendrycks grinned. He had big, honest teeth. "When you told my sergeant you were here to help Mal Hunter, I thought maybe you might have something to tell *me* where to find him."

He closed the door gently after him.

2

Barney had breakfast the next morning in the dining room of the Omega Hotel. The sun was warm. The air was soft. Every rocking chair on the veranda was occupied by the spectator brigade. From the blue lake came the racket of outboard motors and the distant shouts of water skiers. The waitress was trim and friendly. The breakfast was enormous, well prepared, well served. He was tremendously hungry.

Omega was the county seat. There was a big public square with the usual Civil War monument and a wheeled .75 installed by the VFW in 1920. There were benches, brick walks, a fountain, iron-spiked fencing all around. In the center was the courthouse. To the right was the Omega Times news office, a big wooden building with a false veneer of brick. Behind the newspaper office was a gray, monstrous Victorian house.

Two men had followed Barney from the moment he stepped off the hotel veranda and walked into town. They had not been difficult to spot among the rocking-chair brigade. They stood out from the other guests like mambo dancers in a stately minuet. One was short and fat, the other was young, nervous, pale. They wore a gaudy assortment of sport clothes they thought suitable to a mountain resort. Barney was interested. He was not troubled by them. He let them follow as he crossed the central square and went into the newspaper office.

There was no difficulty in getting the elderly woman

clerk to let him browse through the files. He found a comfortable chair in the sunlight next to a window in the rear, facing the lawn and the big Victorian house in back, and read about Malcolm Hunter.

There were photographs: a big man, over six feet, with a fine narrow head, cruel mouth, an arrogance in the black eyes that frowned at the camera. Even in the spotty news photo, an aura of money and power touched Barney. There were pictures of Malcolm Hunter playing polo, Hunter in night clubs, Hunter at Cannes. He'd been snapped at the Governor's inaugural, at the dedication of the new high school, the opening of a wing to the Omega Public Library, the unveiling of a statue in the courthouse to Colonel Mauritius Hunter of the Continental Army that fought at Bennington, Vermont. There were pictures of Hunter in his private plane, in his Jaguar, aboard the racing schooner Clio in the annual Bermuda races. It formed a fairly thorough pattern.

There had been two marriages, one to a wispy New York deb named Georgette Freeley. Nothing was said about how she had been disposed of. There was only one story on the second marriage, to an Evelyn Smith of Reading, Pa. No background on Miss Smith. No further details. Presumably, she still lived in the sprawling English Tudor estate up at the head of the lake.

A sister existed in Paris, apparently in exile. The much older brother, Jan, was relegated to New York, and Barney had already met Jan. He was almost through with his research when he heard an apologetic cough at his elbow.

"Mr. Forbes?"

He looked up into a pair of soft, sad brown eyes in a narrow, effeminate face. The man said: "I'm Jase Franklyn. I'm the editor of the Omega Times."

They shook hands. Franklyn was the fluttery type. He wore a black linen suit with a prissy blue polka-dot bowtie. He looked studious, with a white goatee and an intellectual forehead.

"You are interested in Mal Hunter, I understand."

"You have a fine grapevine in Omega," Barney said.

Hands fluttered up, down, sidewise. "Jake Hendrycks mentioned you. You won't find anything in those clippings, Mr. Forbes."

"Hunter gets fine coverage in your newspaper."

"Not my paper, Mr. Forbes. It once was. When Mother owned it. The Omega Times now belongs to Malcolm Hunter."

"Like everything else in Omega?"

A weak smile, more fluttering of hands that nevertheless closed firmly on the big book of clippings and replaced it on the dusty shelf. "I'm sorry, Mr. Forbes. We can't help you."

"Are you afraid of Hunter, too?" Barney prompted.

"Not exactly. I have other interests now. I am writing a history of Omega in Colonial times. This is an interesting part of the country in that respect. No one has ever done it justice. I've been working on my history of Omega for seven years."

Barney looked through the window at the Victorian house in the rear. There were fine old oaks and maples, hedges that had grown rank and wild, peeling paint on the scroll and jigsaw work on porches and cupolas. Two copper deer stood in green splendor on the weedy lawn. Seated on the sagging porch steps, looking up at him as he stood at the window, were the two men who had followed him from the lakefront hotel.

They sat in the hot sun. The fat one mopped his face with a lavender handkerchief. The younger man nervously smoked a cigarette. They looked as if they wished they were back in some Broadway air-conditioned bar.

"Friends of yours?" Barney asked.

"Dear me, no."

"Who lives there?"

"I do. It was Mother's house. I've always lived there."

"Are those men waiting to see you?"

"I can't imagine why," Franklyn said. His thin, ivory face was covered with a faint dew of perspiration. His soft brown eyes were frightened. "I really must ask you to leave, Mr. Forbes."

"No more research permitted?"

"I'm sorry."

"I'll see you again, perhaps. I'd like to read your history of Omega."

The hands fluttered. "Oh, but that would be impossible. After all, if you are leaving town today—"

"But I'm not leaving," Barney said. "I'm looking for Malcolm Hunter."

"He is not in Omega."

"How do you know?"

"Why, everybody says he's gone. After that trouble with young Alex Kane. But he'll be back, of course. I wouldn't want him to think that *I* caused him any trouble. I hope you understand, Mr. Forbes."

"Then you are afraid of him," Barney said. "I understand that."

"Afraid?" The hands stopped fluttering. The little goatee stopped quivering. Briefly, Jason Franklyn's face and manner changed. He said something in his soft, effeminate voice that Barney did not quite catch, but which sounded obscene.

"I am not afraid of Malcolm Hunter. I hate him. He robbed me of everything dear to me in this life. He caused Mother's death when he took over the newspaper. Why shouldn't I hate him?"

He stood looking down at the two men on the porch steps, but he wasn't really seeing them. Whatever he was looking at, it was beyond Barney's ability to see, also. There was a soft rumble of presses being started somewhere in the building, but Franklyn did not hear that, either. Barney started to speak, then put on his coat and went out.

Franklyn did not turn to say goodbye. The gray woman clerk at the desk behind the office rail looked at him quickly, pursed her mouth, and returned to her work.

As he went out, Barney seemed to hear the soft thud of another door being closed against him.

3

He knocked on other doors that morning.

Leaving the newspaper office, he crossed the tree-shaded square to the courthouse. The benches were crowded, there was a moderate press of traffic. Pigeons fluttered and lit and fluttered up again. Squirrels gorged on peanuts. The sun was hot, the shade of the oaks cool and peaceful.

The two men sauntered after him on the brick walk to the courthouse.

He knocked on the door of District Attorney Hiram Straehle. Straehle was one of those small, energetic men with popping eyes and steel-rimmed glasses who give the impression of being impatient with all the frivolities of life. He wore a dark blue business suit and a fine silk four-in-hand and he sweated even with the droning fan blowing air over him. More pigeons rumbled and cooed on the granite window sill.

Straehle listened with thin lips that grew thinner as Barney spoke. Then he said in a metallic voice: "There is nothing here for you, Forbes. I have not ordered an investigation because there is nothing to investigate. We have no evidence of foul play anywhere."

"What about Ferne Kane's statement?"

"Nonsense. The girl seeks sensations."

"She says Mal Hunter fought with and killed Alex Kane."

"We have no evidence. No body."

19

"Have you looked?"

"Why should we?"

"Have you been in touch with Malcolm Hunter?"

Straehle said: "This is not a police state, Forbes." He looked regretful for a moment, as if he wished it were. "We have no jurisdiction over the comings and goings of anyone not a known criminal."

"Hunter has been charged by Kane's wife with a criminal act. A slight case of murder."

"Are you working for Hunter?" Straehle asked.

"His brother hired me."

Straehle tried to smile. It was too much for him. "Jan Hunter has no money. He lives on an allowance Malcolm doles out to him, perhaps simply to keep him in club funds and theater tickets in New York. Jan Hunter is of no consequence."

"But Malcolm is?"

"In Omega, yes."

"Can he get away with murder?"

Straehle stood up. The pigeons fluttered off the window ledge. His voice was savage. "Forbes, I checked up on you this morning. You're a snooper, hired by a weak-minded man who sees ogres under every bush. I am perfectly capable of handling anything that needs attention here. I advise you to forget about the matter and go home."

"Has Alex Kane any family?"

Straehle looked surprised. "No. Just his wife."

"So nobody really misses him, is that it?"

"You son of a bitch," Straehle grated. "Are you looking for trouble?"

"My job is to find Hunter. Maybe he doesn't want to be found. When I locate him, I'm supposed to help him. Maybe he doesn't want to be helped. Everybody in Omega seems ready to fall over each other in their willingness to lend Mal Hunter a hand. Maybe I'm wasting

my time. For my money, I'd rather be working for Alex
Kane, sight unseen. But I'm getting paid for this, and I
intend to follow it through. Is that clear, Mr. Straehle?"

"Get out of my office."

Barney said: "You're going to have to talk to me sooner
or later. You're going to have to help me find Alex Kane
and Malcolm Hunter."

Straehle's mouth drained white, puckered. "Do you
want me to put you under arrest right now?"

"On what charge?"

"I can think of several, easily enough."

"And have Peterman, Klassen, Smith, Woolley and
Smith on your neck?" Barney asked. This was a bluff.
He knew that at the slightest hint of legal difficulty, he
would be cut adrift and disowned. He said: "I think
you're covering something. I think you're sheltering
Malcolm Hunter, because he owns you, body and soul,
like he seems to own everybody up here."

"And he owns you," Straehle sneered. "You're working
for him, aren't you?"

"Up to a point."

"With Mal Hunter, you go all the way with him, or
you go down the drain. Which is exactly why you ought
to be making tracks for the railroad station, Forbes. Go
back to town and tell that soft-headed Jan Hunter that
Mal won't thank him for interfering."

"Then I get no help from you?" Barney asked.

"You get the boot, snooper."

"Well, thanks for your courtesy," Barney said.

He went out.

The door slammed violently behind him.

Barney walked thoughtfully across the square, with its
bench-warmers and pigeons and squirrels. The fat man
and the nervous man appeared behind him. They looked
unhappy about their job. He was angry enough to double
back and confront them, but it would be interesting to

give them rope. He walked on with his thoughts, frowning in the hot sun.

It was ten o'clock in the morning. He found a garage and was sent from there to a Chevrolet agency and rented a small tan coupe, two years old. He took his time inspecting it. The fat man stood wearily in the shade of an awning across the road; the young, nervous one disappeared. When Barney thought he had given them enough time, he closed the deal and drove north out of Omega.

He followed the shore of the lake. The asphalt road became gravel, then a simple dirt trail that wound along the pine-clad peninsulas that thrust green fingers into the aching blue water. Now and then he glimpsed a panoramic view down the length of the lake, south to the hotel. There were rustic cottages along the waterfront, with here and there a more pretentious summer home. The air seemed kissed with wine.

Behind him, in the dust of his rented car, a green sedan clung doggedly to his trail. In it were the fat man and the nervous man.

Lily would have liked Omega, Barney thought. He remembered how she had looked in a sharkskin bathing suit, golden skin glowing with health, her red mouth laughing, her gray eyes soft and gentle. The twist of pain in him was as sharp as it had ever been. It had been a dream, a fantasy, that house on the Sound, everything new and crisp, even the shining new car, that damned new car. . . .

Stop it, he told himself.

He came at last to where the sign said *Arrow Cove* and turned into a rutted road that led directly to the lake shore. The other car followed, then dropped out of sight.

Alex Kane's place was a rustic lodge, with a screened porch overlooking the lake, a small dock, and another

shed building down on the rocks with a luncheonette
sign on it. Barney tried to remember what he had been
told about Kane—a Korean war veteran, a native of
Omega, who had saved his pay, received the Bronze
Star and a cluster for gallantry, came home, married the
town tart, and set himself up in business, catering to the
boaters on the lake in summer and hunters in the fall.

The luncheonette was closed now. No vacationers in
canoes or outboards crowded the dock for a coke and
hamburger. Barney got out of the car, careful not
to slam the door. He heard the swift trickle of water from
a stream that fell white over the rock ledge behind the
house and foamed into the lake. A bluebird made a
flash of color against green cedars. The sky was like a
crystal bubble. A squirrel scolded him as he walked to
the house.

A radio crooned from beyond the screened door.
Barney let himself silently into a pine-paneled kitchen
where the unwashed dishes were piled high in the sink.
Ashtrays overflowed with carmine-tipped cigarettes.
Field mice had nibbled at a flour bag and caused a small
stream of white to spill over the counter. The radio
played on. He held his hand out to stop the screened
door from slamming, then crossed the tiled floor.

The living room was comfortable, with large windows
facing the lake for most of the wall, then yielding to a
screened porch. The mountains looked unreal, far out
there. On the paneled wall was a crude oil painting
hung over the fieldstone fireplace. The hearth overflowed
with ashes that nobody had bothered to clean up. There
were bright Indian blankets over the couch. A lamp lay
toppled that also had proved too much bother for someone to straighten. The empty liquor bottle beside it had
been picked up once too often.

The music came from the screened porch. Barney
crossed the braided rugs toward it. He heard a clicking

sound and did not recognize it and then he stepped out onto the high porch and saw that the girl there was snapping her fingers in time to the music.

She wore white shorts and a bra of toweling and she lay on her back on a cot, her long, tanned legs propped up against the wall, her head hanging over the edge of the cot. Her blonde hair reached to the floor. Bracelets jangled on her wrists. Her eyes were closed and her orange mouth smiled dreamily.

"Mrs. Kane," Barney said.

Her eyes popped open, the smile jolted into a dark circle of shock, the long legs came down and around in a flashing arc and she was on her feet, facing him.

"Cripes, you scared me!"

"I'm sorry. Perhaps I should have knocked."

"You're damned right you should have knocked! Look, we're closed. No more business. Take your boat and get your beer someplace else, huh?"

"I didn't come for beer. I want to talk to you, Mrs. Kane."

She breathed deeply. She trembled for a moment, then reached down behind the cot and picked up a bottle, shook it, heard it tinkle to her satisfaction. Then she took a long drink from it. Then she stopped for breath and lowered her head; her pale green eyes were angry slits, and her mouth curved sullenly.

"Are you a cop?"

"I'm a lawyer, Mrs. Kane."

"I don't need a cop and I got less need for a lawyer. Beat it."

"I'm looking for your husband," Barney said.

The slitted eyes popped wide, narrowed again. "Why?"

"I heard Alex got himself killed."

"Then you heard it right."

"Where is he?"

"How would I know? In the woods. Up in the mountains. In the lake. I don't know."

"Sit down, Mrs. Kane. You're going to talk to me."

"To hell with you."

"There's no reason why we can't be friends," Barney said.

She studied him carefully, slowly, from head to foot. She thought about him, frowning. She looked at him again. Her laughter was sudden, thin and wiry, surprising because he expected a softer, deeper sound from her magnificent body. She shook her long blonde hair into place. Slowly, as she made up her mind, her body relaxed. She sat down deliberately, emphasizing the curve of her hip. She took a deep breath and touched her chin with the point of her finger. A smile curved the orange lips.

"What's your name?" she asked.

"Barney Forbes."

"You've never been here before, have you?"

"No. I'm from New York."

"Some day I'm going to New York," she said. "I could've gone before I married Alex, but I always figured that when I go it will be in real style, y'know? With money in the bank and clothes on my back to make 'em sit up and take notice of Ferne. It won't be long now, either. I'm so sick of this place, I could spit."

"It's a nice place," Barney said.

"You think so? That's what Alex always said. He built it himself." She forgot her provocative smile and sneered. "A regular little home-maker, that was Alex."

"What makes you so sure that he's dead?"

"I'm sure, all right."

"But why? Did you see him get killed?"

"No," she said sullenly.

He asked evenly: "Are you expecting a great deal of money soon?"

"You bet I am. I—" She broke off, chagrined. "What kind of a crack is that supposed to be?"

"You said you expected to go to town with a bundle."

"Well, I meant Alex's life insurance."

"I see."

"Don't you believe me?"

"Nobody in town seems to believe you, Ferne."

"You've been talking to all those stuffy bastards in Omega," she said hotly. "They all hate me. But you don't have to listen to them. I could tell you plenty. I could tell them all off. But I won't. Not until the time is right."

Barney picked up the bottle of rye and carried it with him into the kitchen. He paid no attention to the girl's angry protest. He found two glasses in the litter of china that filled the sink, rinsed them carefully, and carried them back to the screened porch. The girl now sat in a striped chair, her back to the lake. She had her legs crossed. One foot swung angrily.

"You make yourself at home, don't you?"

"Why not? We'll get along."

"You take a lot for granted."

He poured two drinks, handed her one, tasted his own. The rye was cheap and warm. Ferne Kane drank quickly and greedily. Yet there was a shrewdness in her narrow face, a sense of waiting. She never took her eyes off him. Wasps banged against the screens, and from far off down the lake came the sputtering and racketing of outboard motors. Then for a time there was silence and he heard the serene tinkling of the brook behind the house.

"Who are you working for, Barney?" she asked abruptly.

"Malcolm Hunter."

It jolted her. Her drink spilled down over the thrust of her toweled breasts. Her mouth was ugly. Then she laughed, a bit uneasily. "You must be kidding!"

"No, I'm not."

She said sharply: "Did Mal send you to make a deal?"

"What kind of a deal?"

"You know," she said.

"You'd better tell me all about it," Barney suggested. "Then we'll all know where we stand."

She considered this and she considered the bottle of rye. Deciding to hell with it, she poured herself another drink. The sun was hitting the porch now, and Barney felt its heat strike him, bouncing up off the surface of the lake in a thousand sparkling lances of light.

"It's no secret that Mal likes me," the girl said. "He was always hanging around here, up to last week, on some excuse or other. Alex thought it was great that Hunter was his friend. But Alex was just too stupid to see that the real reason Mal came around so much was because he couldn't keep his hands off me." She sounded complacent.

"How do you feel about Mal?"

"He's rich, y'know?"

"Is that all?"

"That's enough," she said bluntly. "Rich."

"And married," Barney said.

"That never stopped him from fooling around whenever he felt like fooling."

"What happened here the night both men disappeared?"

"Mal came over in the evening, as usual, in his launch. Had some beer in the shack down there. That's all we're allowed to sell—beer. It's a town ordinance. But then he'd always come up here and pretend to talk to Alex, but all the time he kept putting his hands on me. We both knew what the score was—Mal and me, y'know? But Alex was just too dumb and blind. He thought Mal just came to talk about the war and his plane."

"Whose plane?" Barney asked.

"Mal's, of course. It's gone, now, though."

"With Mal?"

"I guess so. Anyway, he was here talking to Alex last Tuesday night, looking at me all the time, and I guess he drank a little too much. He got careless." The blonde girl looked smug now. She pushed up her long hair, arched her body for Barney's benefit, then slumped down again. "Alex suddenly caught on to what was happening. Alex is part Indian, like Charley Danger, over across the lake. Alex always had a terrible temper, but he never showed it like he did that night." She paused, leaned forward, letting the towel slip. "Would you like another drink?"

"Later, Ferne. Go on, please."

"You're cute, you know that?" She laughed. "You think you're kidding me? You think I'm stupid, don't you?"

"Go on," he said.

"Have you got a girl, Barney?"

"No."

"Would you like me to be your girl?"

"Later," Barney said. "We'll take it up later."

"You bastard. You think you're so smart."

"You're Mal Hunter's girl," Barney said. "That's good enough for me. What happened when your husband caught on to Mal's interest in you?"

"They had a fight. Alex tried to kill Mal. They went fighting all over the place, smashing up the furniture, rolling down the steps, out there on the rocks." Ferne Kane's eyes shone with relish, remembering the scene. "They were like a couple of wild animals, y'know? I never saw anything like it." She shivered with pleasure. "They almost killed each other, because of me. Anyway, Mal almost killed Alex. He beat him up something awful."

"Didn't you try to stop it?" Barney asked.

"Why should I?"

"It's a nice question. Was anybody else here who saw them fighting?"

"No. It was late by then. There were no customers down in the shack." She leaned forward again. Her eyes glistened with sudden greed. "Come on, Barney. Don't keep me in suspense. What is Mal offering?"

"What would you like?" Barney asked.

"Well, after all, I saw it. He could get the chair, if I signed a statement, if I testified. He owes me plenty."

"Tell me the rest of it, first."

"There is no more," she said, sulky now. "Mal left in his launch and I went down and found Alex all bloody, beaten to a pulp. I helped him in here and put him to bed. The next morning he was gone."

"Where did he go?"

"He said he got a call for a guided party up at Moon Cove. That's where he *said* he was going. But he never came back. You can guess who really called him up there. It was Mal. And Mal killed him up there."

Barney let air out of his lungs softly. "That's not evidence, Ferne. That doesn't prove anything. Did you see Mal after that night, though?"

"No."

"Have you heard from him?"

"Sure," she grinned. "You showed up, didn't you?"

"I have no authority to offer you anything," Barney said.

"Then why are you here?"

He was silent. She looked at him, her gray-green eyes challenging, then puzzled. Fear dawned in them slowly. She touched her upper lip with the tip of her pink tongue. She looked at the bottle, then jerked her glance away, deciding she'd had enough. Something ugly crawled over her face.

"No money?" she whispered.

"You don't have anything on Malcolm Hunter that

would stand up for a second in court," Barney said.

"Oh, you rotten—"

He stood up. "I'll be back soon," he said. "When I've found Mal Hunter and your husband."

"Don't come back!" she screamed. "You do and I'll kill you! Tell Mal when you see him that I'm going to talk my head off! Tell him that! And tell him I won't take less than double what I asked for before! He can come crawling to me on his hands and knees, he can come begging, and I won't listen! You dirty—"

Leaving the house by the kitchen door, he started toward his parked car. The two men from the green sedan were standing there in the sunlight, waiting for him.

4

THE FAT one mopped his face and coughed apologetically. The nervous one flipped away a cigarette into the
grass, where it lifted a thin plume of blue smoke. The
squirrels scolded noisily, the brook babbled, the lake
made little lapping sounds on the pebbly shore. A peaceful world. Barney walked toward the two men.

"Forbes?" said the fat man.

"You ought to know by now," Barney said. The fat
man wore a yellow nylon sport shirt with an open collar
over a gray gabardine suit. His suede shoes had thick
rope soles. He had a shiny saddle nose and small, knowl-
edgeable eyes and a purse of a mouth. "Why the tail
job?" Barney asked.

"We do what we're told. Now we're calling time on
you," said the young, thin one.

"So?"

"We'll take you to the railroad station," said the fat
man. "Henry, you take it easy. This man is reasonable.
He knew we were tailing, but he didn't mind. It shows
a willingness to cooperate. It shows we're not goin' to
have any trouble with him at all."

"That's what you think," Barney said. Both men were
armed. Their guns were poorly concealed under their
sport coats. They were two-bit hoodlums, picked up in
some Broadway backwash, and they were floundering in
this mountain environment like fish out of water. "Who
hired you?"

31

"Let's say we both work for the same party."

"Hunter?"

"Let's say you've been fired." The fat man smiled again, apologetically. He wiped his face with his limp handkerchief. "Let's say our mutual employer doesn't care to have you snooping for his brother, hey? So you take the 12:12 back to the big city, and I wish I was goin' with you, Forbes."

"Let's say I don't go," Barney said.

The young, nervous one snapped: "You want trouble?"

"That's what I was sent to find."

"Then you've got it. Right here and now."

"Easy, Henry," warned the fat man.

"Stop bubbling. I told you from the start, he don't look right. He was a cop. Wasn't you, Forbes? A big, tough cop. Now he's with the law books and the legal lumps. But a cop stays a cop all his life. Like a disease, it is." Abruptly the nervous one said: "Ah, come on. Let's go."

He reached into a pocket for his gun. Barney hit him with a short left, saw him double forward, and chopped at the gun that bloomed in the fat man's hand. The fat man was surprisingly quick. He slid aside, away from the parked car, and danced back across the grass on tiny, agile feet. The gun he held was a P-38. The warm sunlight was blotted up by its vicious black shape.

"Hold it now. Just hold it. Don't flip," said the fat man.

Barney looked at the younger one sitting on the grass, holding his stomach and retching. The man's face was white and strained. His eyes were black pieces of glass shining up at Barney. He looked at his companion and saw that the fat man had his gun on Barney and he grinned crookedly and struggled to his feet.

"This will be for kicks."

"Stay back, Henry," said the fat man.

"Like hell. I owe the snooper a fast dance."

Henry came in lightly, something metallic shining in his hand. He swung, and Barney ducked, hit him again, threw him toward the fat man. The fat man's gun went off with an explosive crash. Barney dived over the stumbling Henry and hit the fat man with his shoulder, bowling him over. The gun blasted again at the sky. The fat man squawked in high terror. A few leaves came drifting down from the arched trees overhead. Barney wrenched the P-38 free, rolled away, bounced to his feet. The younger man sat on the grass, sobbing in rage. The fat man sighed, wiped his face with the handkerchief.

"That didn't go at all well," he whispered.

"You're a couple of amateurs," Barney said. "You'd do better without Henry, here. He's too eager."

"I have to teach him," said the fat man.

Barney went over to Henry and plucked his gun away. Then he walked down to the lake front and threw both weapons as far as he could into the calm, sparkling water. They made twin splashes, far out beyond Alex Kane's boat landing. He looked up at the screened porch and saw Ferne standing there, leaning eagerly forward. When she saw that he was in one piece, she looked disappointed. He laughed silently and returned to the two hoodlums.

"Who hired you?" he asked again.

They were silent.

He considered them for a moment, wondering if it was worth the effort to make them talk. He had much to do. They were not important, he decided. They stood side by side, looking their mute enmity at him. The next time they met, Barney knew, they would be more dangerous. But maybe there would be no other meeting. Turning, he left them as they were and got into his car and drove away.

There was a public phone booth beside the road back

to the Omega Hotel. Barney parked in front of a cedar
rail and found enough change to call New York. He gave
the number of Peterman, Klassen, Smith, Woolley and
Smith, lit a cigarette, and waited. He heard the telephone
ringing distantly, and in his mind he saw the sombre,
oak-paneled office with its hunting prints, its tiers of
law books, the enormous desk, and the elf seated behind
the desk. Jeremy Peterman, the senior partner and the
only one Barney had met, was a tiny man whose feet
never quite touched the floor when he sat behind that
huge desk. He was seventy, white-haired, shrewd, a
genius at trusts. He had handled Barney, as Barney remembered, with the attitude of someone forced to deal
with a rather clumsy aborigine.

He got the receptionist, was advised to wait, told her
it was the firm's money being wasted, and was promptly
connected with Peterman. The little man had a surprisingly deep voice.

"Forbes? Why are you calling?"

"I think I'm going to quit," Barney said.

"What?"

"I'm not needed up here," Barney said. "Malcolm Hunter has all the help he can use. Everybody from the D.A.
on down is anxious to help him. They're falling all over
themselves here in Omega to cover up whatever they
think Hunter did. I have the nasty feeling that I'm
working on the wrong side of the fence."

"Nonsense, my boy. Stay with it. Have you discovered
anything pertinent?"

"Just what I've told you. It adds up, though. I think
Alex Kane is dead and I think Malcolm Hunter killed
him and I think the whole town knows damned well that
Hunter did it."

"This sort of problem is somewhat out of our line,"
Peterman said faintly. "It is not the sort of thing we are
accustomed to coping with."

"Naturally. That's why you hired me. It's not quite respectable."

The telephone hummed. A bee banged against the phone booth door and butted the glass angrily and then gave up. Two fat women in flowered shorts came down the road on wobbling bicycles. Their faces were red and perspired and determined. When they were gone, Barney said: "The whole set-up is a little rank. I've been argued with, threatened, cajoled, ordered and invited to take the first train back to New York. I don't like it. Just because of that, I'd rather stay here, but I don't quite see what I can do."

"Have you seen Mrs. Hunter yet?"

"I tried last night. I didn't get past the watchman's gate. But I'll try again."

"Good," said Peterman. "I am a little uneasy about the aspect of the police being involved. Under no account are you to embroil this firm in unfavorable publicity. Do you understand?"

"Nuts," Barney said.

"Eh? What?"

"You hired me to do a job. I'll do it. I'll find Malcolm Hunter for his brother, and if he needs help of any kind, I'll give it to him, short of covering up murder. If any of the chips bounce, I can't help it. Murder seldom leaves everybody with clean skirts."

"You're rather blunt, Forbes."

"I mean to be."

"Well, well. I trust you will use every discretion to avoid unpleasant notice in this matter. I have a clue for you, as I believe you might call it. Mr. Jan Hunter, our client, received a call this morning from an Indian, a Mr. Charles Danger, who was Malcolm's pilot until very recently. He was discharged two weeks ago. Danger phoned to say he had some information that may be useful. I would suggest that you see him at once."

"All right. About our esteemed client, though. Everyone here in Omega seems surprised that Jan should dream of interfering with his brother's problems. It seems that Jan is held in mild contempt by everyone who knows of him. I've been wondering where our client got the nerve to retain me to poke into Malcolm's disappearance. And an obvious answer has occurred to me."

"I am interested," said Peterman calmly.

"You might ask Jan one question. Ask him if he got his courage to interfere in Malcolm's affairs because he knows that Malcolm is already dead."

"My word!" Peterman was shocked. "Is he?"

"I'm betting on it," Barney said.

"See here." There was a pause. "See here. Please, Forbes. Do what you can. And try to avoid any peccadilloes."

"Peccadilloes," Barney said. "Yes."

"Precisely."

Barney hung up.

5

The Hunter estate sprawled on the west shore of the lake, a rambling Tudor house with exposed beams, slate roofs, many gables. There was a velvety green lawn, rhododendrons, a formal garden, a high iron fence surrounding the acreage. The lawns sloped down to the lake front with a miniature of the manor house serving as a boat shed. There was a thirty-foot cabin cruiser, and moorings for a plane. There were terraces with striped umbrellas, a fine imported sand beach, towering oaks and spruce, and an air of desolate emptiness as Barney was admitted through the high iron gate and drove up the winding drive.

A man waited, scowling in the sun, on the terrace between carefully trimmed privet hedges. The man remained where he was while Barney walked up the shallow flagstone steps toward him.

"Forbes? I'm Felix Branthorpe. Estate manager."

They did not shake hands. Branthorpe was about thirty, medium height, with enormously wide shoulders, a flat, tanned face. His blond hair was cropped in a stiff brush, close to his skull. He gave an impression of physical power that was not lessened by his thin voice. His eyes were a cool, hostile gray.

"I told Mrs. Hunter about you. I advised her that you would come here and I also advised her not to see you. But she insists that you be given a chance to say your piece. For my part, you're not welcome here."

"Since when does your job as estate manager give you the right to pick and choose Mrs. Hunter's visitors?"

Branthorpe flushed. A muscle jumped in his heavy jaw. "I'm a friend and adviser of the family, as well as an employee. My sole interest is in protecting Malcolm Hunter's property."

"By way of keeping his wife incommunicado?"

Branthorpe's hands closed into fists. "I didn't say that."

"I think you'd better get out of my way," Barney said. "Go stand in front of a mirror and make muscles at yourself. I'm too busy to argue."

Branthorpe's rage was poorly concealed. For a moment, Barney thought the man would not move. He weighed well over two hundred and from his lightly balanced stance Barney guessed he would not be easy to handle, one way or the other. He was in no mood for unnecessary trouble. He looked at Branthorpe's glacial eyes and the man stared at the lake, jerked his square jaw to the left, and said: "On the back terrace."

"You first, Felix," Barney said.

The man's mouth curled. Then he turned and went up the shallow steps three at a time. The tall Gothic doors of the house stood open to the lake breeze. There was an entrance hall of red Belgian tiles, a huge stone fireplace with carved griffins standing guard, and suits of armor in wall niches. On the paneling was a collection of hunting bows, old English longbows, arquebuses, crossbows of every size, including one that was distinctly Chinese, inset with an intricate ivory design. Branthorpe's shoes made no sound at all as he led the way through the house, past a tall stained-glass window, and through French doors to a terrace in the rear.

A hedge of yellow Pinocchio roses made a splash of color against tidy yews and arbor vitae. The slate terrace came in subdued pastels. The bees were busy. Under a candy-striped umbrella was a redwood lounge chair with an aquamarine sun mattress lashed to it with yellow cords. Branthorpe spoke in a harsh voice. "Jan's snooper is here, Evelyn."

The woman on the lounge chair said: "Thank you, Felix. You can leave us alone."

"I'd rather not," Branthorpe said. His neck was red. "Please, Felix."

"Mal wouldn't like it."

"Mal isn't here. Do as I say."

Branthorpe hesitated, eyes hot and furious. His fists clenched, then his hands went slack. He turned on his heel, his shoe making a brief squealing sound on the tiled terrace, and slammed back into the house.

Barney stood as he was. For a moment, when he first saw the back of the woman's head, the length of her legs, he felt an unholy pounding in his heart against his ribs, a quick tremor and a frantic denial shouting in the back of his mind. It was as if he were seeing Lily again. The way she held her head, the same trick of tying a blue ribbon in her hair, the way she lay with her long legs outstretched. The same silky shine of black hair, shoulder-length, the same deep, calm voice. He was badly shaken.

Then he walked around to take a chair where he could look clearly into her face. She wore dark sunglasses with jeweled bows like butterfly wings. She wore a yellow sunsuit the color of melted butter, with big ivory buttons. Her face was the same, yet not the same. He felt relieved and then he felt disappointed and then he told himself to put it out of his mind. Lily was dead. He could not go on seeing her every now and then in various women he met or passed. She would not have wanted to haunt him so, he told himself.

"What is it, Mr. Forbes?" she asked.

He had not realized he was staring. "You reminded me for a moment of someone I once knew. I'm sorry."

"Sorry I'm not she?" Evelyn Hunter smiled.

"In a way. I'd rather not—"

"Of course. You're the man Jan hired, aren't you, to look after Mal?"

"Yes, I am."

She said: "Jan was always fussy, unable to see the true picture. It is Malcolm who always looks after Jan. Jan means well, I suppose. But he will not be thanked for sending you here. Malcolm has always been able to cope with his own problems."

"I've come to realize that. But this problem may be murder."

"Don't say that."

"It must be said, Mrs. Hunter. Until one or the other or both men turn up. Ferne Kane is crying murder, and it has to be answered."

She was silent. There were tiny beads of perspiration on her short upper lip. Her mouth was soft and Barney received an impression of sadness. When she took off her glasses and he looked at her dark blue eyes, the sadness was still there. She looked defeated, as if something had broken inside her long, long ago.

"I don't like to bother you, Mrs. Hunter," Barney said. He spread his hands. "But I must find your husband and talk to him. If there's nothing to Ferne Kane's story, then I'll be happy to pack up and go home."

"If Ferne says that Mal was trying to sleep with her, I'll believe that," the woman said quietly. She looked at the bank of yellow roses nearby. "I'd believe almost anything about Mal."

"Even murder?"

"It's quite possible."

"Do you think he killed Alex Kane?"

"I don't know what to think, Mr. Forbes. I—I've rather lost the knack of thinking for myself, this past year. If

Mal isn't here to tell me what to do, then Felix is only too eager to take over."

Not like Lily, Barney thought. *Not at all like Lil.* Yet he felt a kinship to her, because of his startled first impression. He knew it was irrational to feel pity for her because of those first words of hers, but he felt sorry, nevertheless, and a quick urge filled him, impelling him to help her. Probably she didn't want help. She had married Mal Hunter as Evelyn Smith, of Reading, Pa. A coal-miner's daughter, perhaps. It happened. There was nothing to feel sorry about. She got what she wanted.

"Have you heard from Mal since the night he disappeared?" he asked.

"No. Nothing."

"Did he come back from Kane's place that night?"

"Oh, yes. It was very late. Two or three o'clock in the morning. He was drunk. He—he was impatient with me because I asked him where he'd been and what he'd been doing." Her mouth curved down. "He left me this to think about." She touched the long silken curve of her thigh. There was a mottled bruise high up near her hip, under the fold of her sunsuit. "Do I shock you, Mr. Forbes?"

"A little," he said.

"You may as well know for whom you are working."

Barney nodded. "Did he say anything at all about where he was going, or why?"

"Nothing. He was in a rage. He took the plane and flew off, after finishing a bottle of liquor."

"He was drunk? This was at night?"

"He can do anything, drunk or sober."

"No pilot?"

"He used to have a man named Charles Danger who flew for him. But Charles was too fine and decent to take the sort of treatment that Mal inflicts upon those who work for him. Charles quit two weeks ago. There was another man. Al Greeley from Jackson, who occasionally acted as an air chauffeur, but Al—I don't know if he was here that night or not."

"And you haven't heard from Mal since."

"No."

A bee hummed around a bottle of suntan lotion on a red-lacquered Javanese table near the lounge chair. Evelyn Hunter put her butterfly glasses back on again. The image of Lily faded from Barney's mind. He watched the woman finger a golden sunburst of intricate design, the center a glowing red stone, on a heavy golden chain around her slender throat. It caught the light, winking and twinkling.

"Where might your husband have gone, Mrs. Hunter?" he asked.

"I couldn't say."

"Meaning you choose not to say?"

"I must consider his wishes in all things."

"Do you think he's alive?"

It startled her. "What do you mean by that?"

"According to Ferne Kane's story, Mal killed Alex Kane. But both men have disappeared. Maybe it happened the other way around. Maybe Alex killed your husband."

She frowned delicately, her brows delicate dark arcs over big, limpid eyes. It was obviously a new thought to her.

"It's hard to believe that Mal might be dead."

"But not impossible."

She bit her lip. There was no other sign of panic, regret or desperate love. "I must think about that, Mr. Forbes. It must be considered."

He stood up. "Then you can't help me in any way?"

"I'm sorry. No."

He left a few minutes later, walking through the big manorial house. He paused a moment to admire again the collection of crossbows on the wall, flanking the fireplace with its huge stone griffins. Felix Branthorpe appeared in the entrance hall. He had changed from sport clothes to a business suit of subdued Palm Beach gray. His clipped head looked alert, his whole figure carried lightly, easily, on perfectly toned muscles. He walked silently to where Barney stood.

"I'll escort you to the gate. In case you lose your way."

Barney looked at him. "Have you heard from your two stooges yet?"

Branthorpe's head tilted a little to one side. He smiled. His pale eyes were cool. "You're jumping to conclusions," he said softly.

"You know about them, so I wouldn't say I'd stabbed you in the dark. They invited me to take the next train back to town. It was not the first invitation I received today. I told them I regretted it, but I'm staying in Omega."

"And?" still softly.

"You should have hired men who are professionally a bit more adept at their trade, Felix."

The man's neck grew red again. "You're not wanted here, Forbes. Hasn't that been made clear enough?"

"It's nice to find a man so intensely devoted to the interests of his employer," Barney said. "And so intent on guarding his employer's property—including his wife."

Without warning, Branthorpe swung. Barney partially blocked the blow, but the man's strength was like that of a bull. His fist drove in like a sledge, hammering into Barney's middle. Barney slammed against the wall, bounced off it, caught his balance, and ducked under the next swing. He came forward, and suddenly saw that Branthorpe had dropped his guard. His hands were at his sides. His head was cocked as he looked at someone beyond Barney.

He drew in a deep breath and said tightly: "Yes, Evelyn?"

"You're a fool, Felix. Let Mr. Forbes go."

Barney looked at her. She stood at the head of the hall, a striped cape thrown over her slender shoulders. The butterfly glasses dangled from her slim fingers. Her face was scornful. Felix Branthorpe swallowed his rage, ducked his cropped head in a nod, and walked away. Evelyn Hunter gave Barney a smile that was empty of all meaning and turned to follow her estate manager.

Barney found his own way out to the gate.

6

HE HAD lunch at the hotel, and at two o'clock recovered the rented coupe from its parking slot in the rear and drove north along the lake again, on the east shore. He was not followed this time. The mountains came down more precipitously on this side of the lake, exerting pressure on the twisting road between the pine slopes and the water. There were fewer cottages, and those that had been built were balanced precariously on tall uprights, developing several levels. The road was like a tunnel under the deep, scented green of shaggy cedars, and whenever the sunlight failed to penetrate, the air temperature dropped several chilly degrees.

The road jogged suddenly right to circle a deep, narrow cove, and Barney spotted the trimly painted rural mailbox with the name in Old English lettering: *Charles Danger.* He turned off into a steep, rutted path that made the rented car jounce and squeal in protest.

From the shore the main body of the lake was invisible, cut off by a bend of the cove. With the motor off, Barney heard the sound of the wind high up on the mountaintops. The house stood in quiet solitude, bigger and more comfortable than he had expected. It was built of California redwood, standing on heavy piles, backed up against the steep slope to the rear. A vast window wall reflected the green of the trees and the blue of the water. There was a trimly painted dock with a fifteen-foot runabout and a single-prop, aluminum Luscomb monoplane equipped with dual pontoons moored to a white buoy. Barney listened, and heard no sound.

The door to the lower level stood open. He walked in.

The house was empty. There was a huge living room, comfortable, immaculate, heavily masculine. In the study, Barney paused to look at a framed diploma granting a master's degree in literature to Charles G. Danger. The books were all finely bound volumes, well-read, with slips of paper inserted to mark passages of interest. There was a gun rack on the paneled walls that contained an over-and-under shotgun, a Remington .30-08 pump gun, and several hand guns. They were all clean and well oiled.

When he turned, a tall man stood right behind him, a grappling hook in his hand.

The man said quietly: "Make yourself at home. Pick out a good book to read."

The man stood as tall as Barney, lean and wiry, wearing a sweaty striped singlet and white ducks rolled up over bony knees. His brown feet were bare and glistening with drops of water. He held the wicked-looking five-pronged grapnel easily, swinging it a bit from a length of wet rope in his fingers. Mud dripped from several of the tines and splashed on the waxed oak floor. His face was narrow, too dark to be merely tanned, with coppery cheekbones and stiff, coarse black hair. His eyes were calm. His entire manner was one of ease.

"You must be Charley Danger," Barney said.

"That's right. And you?"

"Barney Forbes."

The Indian did not offer to shake hands. The grappling hook kept swinging in its short, gleaming arc. Danger said: "You're the man that Jan hired?"

"Yes. He said you could help me."

"I can," said Danger. "Come along."

"What were you fishing for?" Barney asked.

The Indian hefted the grappling hook. "Bodies. I think I've got one located. Maybe there is only one. Give me a hand."

His manner was calm, flat, without emotion. Barney followed him out of the house to the dock. A small, flat-bottomed rowboat was tied up near the Luscomb cabin plane. "Is that your ship?" Barney asked.

"Yes."

"I thought it might be Mal Hunter's."

"Mal isn't hiding out here with me, if that's what you're getting at."

"I'm not getting at anything," Barney said. He liked this man. "I'm just looking around."

Danger got into the rowboat. "I guess you've had plenty of advice thrown at you this morning. How many people told you to get out of town?"

"Everybody I spoke to."

"Shall I add to it?"

"Spare me," Barney said. "I'm not leaving."

Danger smiled. It was a brief twitch of thin brown lips, nothing more. His black eyes were empty except for that brief flicker of light in them. Barney stepped into the stern of the rowboat and shoved away from the pier. Danger rowed out into the cove with an easy, practiced stroke.

"Did you see Ferne this morning?" Danger asked.

Barney nodded. "She sticks to her story. She says Mal killed her husband."

"Did you like her?"

"If you like beer and pretzels."

"I used to like beer," Danger said. "I used to like Ferne. That was before Korea. I tried to tell Alex not to marry her, but you can't tell your best friend that he's running around with the town tramp."

Barney said carefully: "Are you close friends with the Kanes now?"

Danger looked at him with bleak eyes. "I could think about that remark for a while and it wouldn't take much to dislike it."

"You don't have to answer."

"Alex and I were in Korea. He saved my life, once. I saved his a couple of times. We built my house together, after we came home."

"And now?"

"Ferne would have liked me to keep coming around. I wanted no part of her. Not after she became Alex's wife."

"You could talk yourself into trouble," Barney said, "Telling this around."

"It's already around. The whole town knows it."

"Do you believe Ferne's story about the fight Alex had with Mal?"

"It's not a matter of believing it, one way or the other. I'll soon know the truth."

The rowboat had been allowed to drift to a small, placid elbow in the cove, from which the main body of the lake could be narrowly seen through a slot in the thick stand of evergreen trees. The water was dead calm, clear and cold. For part of the distance out from the pebbly shore, where granitic boulders loomed gray against the brush, the bottom was plainly visible. Then it shelved off into deeper mud and silt below where the rowboat drifted. A small buoy marked the spot. Danger tied the rowboat to it. His face was grave, unreadable.

"Can you see it?" Danger asked.

Barney looked over the side. Dark shapes moved in wavering patterns twelve feet below the surface of the water. He could make out nothing distinctly.

"What is it?" he asked.

"A body. I spotted it this morning."

"Called the police?"

"Hendrycks? Not yet."

"Who is it?"

"We'll soon know. It's weighted down with stones. I hated to use the hook on it. You can help."

The sunlight made a peaceful glimmering over the calm water. Two robins hopped out on a branch over the water and cocked inquisitive heads at the rowboat. Somewhere nearby a fish jumped, splashing.

Barney said: "Why did Mal Hunter fire you?"

Danger stood up, handed him the end of the grappling rope. "We had a difference of opinion."

"What about?"

"Ferne Kane. I told him to stop bothering her. Hold this."

"You don't care how damaging you make things look for yourself, do you?" Barney asked.

"I haven't anything to hide."

With a deft movement, the Indian dived from the rowboat. He struck the water with scarcely a splash, and the few ripples made by the passage of his body quickly lapped against the shore and were gone. Barney watched his sinuous struggle to reach the bottom. Underwater weeds stirred, waved long fronds in a slow-motion, lazy ballet. Mud roiled up like a dark cloud, obscuring his view. He felt a quick tug on the line in his hand, and paid out some slack. Another tug. The seconds ticked by. The robins took off somewhere on business of their own. A speedboat roared by the entrance to the cove, and the wake came in with long, shallow swells that washed and slapped against the granite boulders on shore.

There was an eruption on the surface and Charley Danger's head popped into view. He blew, snorted, took two strokes, and clung to the gunwale of the boat.

"Haul him up."

Barney could tell nothing from the Indian's face. He pulled gently on the line, met resistance, exerted more strength. Something gave a little, snagged, suddenly yielded. A long, dark shape lifted uncertainly to the surface among the roiled clouds of silt and mud.

"I cut away the rocks," Danger offered from the water.

The body rolled slowly, lazily, and something white that might have been a face came up out of the water and settled back. An arm flapped. Barney saw loosened ropes, a water-logged leather windbreaker ballooning grotesquely, dungarees that might once have been blue but which now looked black. Something metallic, still bright, glittered from the chest of the windbreaker. Dark hair wavered in the water, screening the face.

The body rolled over, exposing shoulders and back. A long feathered shaft was thrust out from between the dead man's shoulder blades.

The rowboat rocked, pitched, and splashed sidewise as Charley Danger hoisted himself out of the water. His cheekbones looked white. He took the line from Barney.

"It looks like he was killed with that arrow in his back," Barney said.

Charley Danger's voice was thick. "Not just any arrow, either. Have you been up to Hunter's house?"

"This noon."

"Did you see the crossbow collection?"

"I saw it," Barney said.

"Well, that's an arrow from one of the crossbows."

Danger sat down on a thwart, leaning forward, his hands clenched between his knees, his head lowered. His breathing was harsh.

Barney said: "Well, which one is it?"

The Indian looked up. Surprise flickered amid the grief in his black eyes. "Don't you know? It's Alex Kane."

7

STRAEHLE did not like it. It was hot and crowded in his office, and a pale thin man acting as police stenographer was taking notes. The pigeons cooed and burbled on the sunlit window sill. It was four o'clock in the afternoon. In addition to Straehle and the male stenographer, there was Chief Hendrycks, Felix Branthorpe, and Charles Danger. Barney sat in a hard wooden chair near the door.

Straehle pulled at his thin lower lip. He was sweating in his blue business suit, and he fixed Barney with a baleful glance from his popping, pale eyes. "What is that man doing here, Hendrycks?"

"Forbes was with Charley when they found Kane's body."

"Get him out of here. This is an official investigation."

Hendrycks said heavily: "Hiram, Mr. Forbes was a witness to the way Charley dragged Alex up from the lake. He can verify what Charley says."

"And you would believe him?" Straehle rasped.

Hendrycks stood his ground like a clumsy, uncomfortable bear. "Why not? He don't know Charley; he don't know any of us. I reckon he'll tell us the truth."

"You're a fool. Throw him out."

Barney spoke quietly: "I'm perfectly willing to go. I don't want to watch this farce any more than I have to. But since I'm an attorney retained by the Hunters, I'll have to report that some of this investigation was kept secret from me, that I was afforded no courtesy, and that

51

Malcolm Hunter's interests were jeopardized by my eviction from this office at this time."

Straehle stared at him. "You don't work for Hunter," he said flatly. "Not for Mal, anyway."

"Don't I?" Barney stood up. He didn't know how far his bluff would carry. "Then I'll see you in court."

He had his hand on the door when Straehle said harshly: "Just a minute." The D.A. turned to Felix. "Do you know this man, Branthorpe? Is he telling the truth?"

"I'm not sure," Branthorpe said. He stood across the room from Charles Danger, wearing a white Palm Beach suit and tan woven shoes with silver buckles. His blond hair glistened with pomade. His square, tanned face was sullen. "Let him stay, Hiram. He can't do any harm."

"Very well. Sit down and keep quiet," Straehle said. He swung sharply away in his swivel chair and stared at Danger. "All right, Charley. Tell us what happened at your place that Tuesday."

"Tuesday?" the Indian asked quietly.

"The night Alex Kane was killed in your cove."

"I don't know that he was killed there. He could have been shot with that arrow anywhere, and then dropped at my front door, so to speak. I didn't hear anything or see anything, if that's what you mean."

"Alex was your friend, wasn't he?"

"Yes."

"And Ferne, too, hey?"

"Once. A long time ago."

"You had an itch for her, Charley. Don't deny it."

The Indian's face was dark and sensitive. "What are you getting at, Straehle?" he asked quietly.

"Alex married your girl, that's what I'm getting at. And she had a chain on you. Everybody knows it. He got in your way. You say Alex was shot with a crossbow, and you're a good bowman. I've seen you at the amateur meets, every September down in Greenham. Damn good. You could have swiped one of Hunter's bows from his collection and shot Alex with it to make it look as if Hunter did it. That would have fitted nicely, since Mal was drunk and forgot himself enough to make a pass at Ferne and they had a little fight over it. You could have figured it made a nice time to get rid of Alex and even up with Mal for firing you."

There was an ivory tint under the Indian's tightly drawn cheekbones. "Alex was my best friend."

"Friends have a way of falling out when a woman becomes involved with them."

"Are you saying I killed Alex?"

"We're going to hold you for it," Straehle said flatly.

Hendrycks made a dim rumbling sound of protest. Nothing much else came out of him. Charley Danger said: "You can't cover up for Hunter by accusing me. The truth will come out, no matter how hard you try to hide it." His voice lifted with anger as he swung toward Chief Hendrycks. "All of you, every man in this town, knows how it was with Mal Hunter and Alex's wife. Everybody knows about the fight they had. Yet you're falling over yourselves to hide the blood on Malcolm Hunter's hands. You're selling him a license to kill—it's murder for sale. You know where he's hiding, waiting for this to blow over—waiting for you to find somebody to take the rap. But I won't be the fall guy. You'll find it won't work—"

"Shut up!" Straehle rasped. He swung to the male steno. "Joe, strike that out."

"It won't do any good," Danger said. "You can't cover it now. And you can't bury it with Alex Kane's body."

The room was hot with crackling tension. It was broken momentarily by a quick rap on the office door. A lab technician came in, wearing a white smock. He held an arrow in his hands—a blunt shaft tipped by cruel

steel barbs, feathered gaily at the notched end with blue
pinions.

"You asked for this as soon as possible, Mr. Straehle,"
the technician said. He looked uncertainly around the
room. "Dr. Damon says that Kane was badly beaten
before he was shot with this arrow. The arrow caused his
death instantly, entered with terrific force between the
fourth and fifth ribs, left side—"

"All right, all right," Straehle said. "Get out."

Hendrycks spoke heavily, addressing the D.A. "Charley
says that's one of the arrows that fits Hunter's crossbows."

"Are any crossbows missing?"

"No."

"It's a red herring," Straehle decided. His face was
pinched and shiny with sweat. He licked his lips. "It's use
was designed to involve Mal Hunter. A clumsy, crude
attempt to incriminate him."

Hendrycks sighed. "Hiram, listen, you can't—"

"Watch your step," Straehle warned.

"Yeah, sure. But even so—"

"Don't be a fool, Jake. We've got the man who did it.
With the right motive. Take Charley down to the cell
block and lock him up. The rest of you clear out of
here." Straehle punched a button savagely, and two cops
showed up with a promptness that indicated they had
been waiting for the summons. "All right, I've got work
to do. Danger, you had better behave, you hear? You've
got a reputation for acting mean sometimes. I'll assign
a lawyer to you, if you like."

The Indian laughed softly, shook off the first cop's
hand, and burrowed in his pocket for a ring of keys. He
tossed the keys to Barney, who caught them without
too much surprise.

"Forbes, there is my house. If you're going to stay in
Omega, you'd do me a favor by staying at my place. I'd

like to have somebody in it just to look after things. Be my guest, eh?"

"You can't—" Straehle began angrily. Then he paused. "I can see you're two of a kind. Watch your step, Forbes, or you'll share a cell with Danger."

Barney weighed the keys in his hand. Danger was looking at him steadily, his eyes trying to tell him something. Barney shrugged and pocketed the keys.

"Thanks for your hospitality, Charley."

He went out behind the cops and the tall, proud Indian.

8

His car was parked where he had left it, in the restricted zone beside the courthouse. Long shadows spread over the little park with the setting sun. A newsboy went by, hawking the Omega Times. The squirrels were still busy on the grass between the benches, and a few neon lights were on over the Omega Cafe, the marquee of the movie house, and Frankie's Bowling Alley. Barney lit a cigarette, drew a deep breath of the crisp, piney air, and got into his car.

Chief Hendrycks slid into the seat beside him from the opposite side. Barney halted with his hand at the ignition lock.

"For a big man, you can move soft," Barney said.

"I hunt a lot, come fall," said Hendrycks. "Mind if I sit and talk with you a minute?"

"It's your town. Or Straehle's. Help yourself."

Hendrycks sighed. "You're pretty touchy, son. No need to take what happened to Charley so personally. He was expecting it. Any fool could see he was willing to be locked up."

"Why?"

"Ain't no figuring on a mind like Charley's. You like the man, huh?"

"Yes, I like him."

"So do I."

"You don't think he killed Alex Kane, do you?" Barney asked.

"I'm not thinking anything at all," Hendrycks said softly. "It's Hiram's baby. You got him a little confused, though. He ain't sure who you're working for now. A man like Hiram likes things neat and tidy, and he won't have a restful night, thinking about you. Are you staying in Omega?"

"I haven't decided," Barney said. "Charley is going to need some help. He didn't kill Alex any more than I did. Would you have arrested him, chief, with what you've got on him?"

"Can't say. Hiram is an ambitious man. He thinks he's got a career in politics, and maybe he has. He got elected with Mal Hunter's money, and now he's figuring on a state post come next November. Mal Hunter can make him or break him. He'll cover for Mal all the way, which is something you won't have to worry about. Seeing Mal has so many friends in Omega ought to make you rest easy, son. You really got no work to do for your client at all."

Barney looked sharply at the white-haired man, but Jake Hendryck's face told him nothing. It was gaunt, pleasant, thoughtful.

"Then Straehle plans to make a three-ring circus out of Kane's murder?" Barney asked.

"Probably. Got lots of tabloid appeal. Two life-long friends fight to the death over sexy girl. Ferne takes good pictures. She'll act it up."

"Straehle is going to fall flat on his face," Barney said.

"Make sure he doesn't fall on you first, son. You got any ideas?"

"Maybe Charley did kill him," Barney said. "Or maybe Mal Hunter did it. Maybe Alex Kane took the bow and arrow and shot himself."

"This is no joking matter, son."

"I'm not laughing about it," Barney said. "I've seen

some raw deals before, but every card that's dealt in
Omega comes from the bottom of the deck."

"Why should you complain? It helps you do your job
of helping Malcolm Hunter."

"Yes, but I don't have to like it," Barney said. "The
way Straehle figures it is much too simple. There are
too many other possibilities to close the book on Danger
like this. There's Ferne, and any other male friends
she might have had. Granted it would be stupid of Mal
Hunter to kill Alex when everybody knew about the
fight they had. It's also stupid of Hunter to run away
and stay away. If he swings so much weight around here,
why hide out? He's got you and Straehle in his pocket.
He's got everybody shaking at the mention of his name.
Why should he run away?"

Hendrycks said softly: "Nobody says he ran away."

"Then where is he? Why hasn't he shown up?"

"It's a good question. Got any more like it?"

"Sure. Why would Charley deliberately bring up Alex's
body, if Charley killed him? Why not let it rot there
under the lake?"

"Go on."

"Ferne says somebody called Alex on Wednesday
morning, the day after he fought with Mal. Whoever it
was, said he wanted to hire him for a guided trip. They
were to meet over at Half Moon Cove—which I gather
is Charley Danger's part of the lake shore. Who called
him there? Would Charley do it, if Charley planned to
kill him?"

Hendrycks reached over and turned on the ignition
key. "Let's go ask Ferne some of them questions. That
is, if you don't mind."

Barney did not mind. They drove north out of Omega,
over the road that was now familiar to him. Chief
Hendrycks lit a bulldog pipe and smoked with apparent
contentment and peace of mind. The lake was alive with

violet evening light, here and there reflecting the ruddy glow of the sun as it dipped below the towering mountains. Only once did Hendrycks speak on the way to the Kane place.

"I've been studying you, Barney, and I can't help wondering what you hope to find in our little town of Omega."

"I'm only here to do a job for a client."

"I don't mean that. We all got jobs to do. Most of us do them right around home. But now and then you get a kind of lost look, like a young pup without a home. Me, I don't pretend to be as smart as lots of folks, but I know people. You look lost, and you look as if you hope to find something right around here."

"Perhaps I will," Barney said.

"Do you know what it is you lost?"

"Yes," Barney said. He thought of Lil. "But I'll never find it again."

"Well, don't stop looking. If you stay in Omega for a time, maybe you'd like to have dinner with my family. That is, if you don't mind eight kids at the table with you."

"I'd like it," Barney said. "Thanks a lot."

They turned into the narrow, rutted road to the lake shore. Dusk had come. The bungalow and the landing looked different, shrouded in shadows, as if the change in perspective had subtly altered something basic about the place. There was silence except for the trickling of the stream on the rocky outcropping behind the house. No radio crooned behind the screens of the porch. The door was locked. Hendrycks trudged down the path to the float and tried the door to the refreshment shed. It was also locked. He pushed slim fingers through his dirty-snow hair.

"Looks like she's gone. Maybe she heard about Alex

and came into town. We might've passed her on the way."

"Or maybe she's on her way to New York," Barney said. "She's a girl with plans."

Hendrycks nodded. "And she's got the equipment to get what she wants," he said softly.

They walked back toward the car. "Who did she play around with—besides Malcolm Hunter and Charley Danger?" Barney asked.

"Ain't a man in town who hasn't looked at Ferne and wondered how it would be to have a girl like her."

"Does that include you?"

"I'm a family man, son. But I looked at her. A man can't help himself."

"Straehle, too?"

Hendrycks grinned. "You're biting down too hard on it, right there."

"Doesn't Straehle have a wife? Or a woman?"

"He's all wrapped up in his ambition. He's been with her once or twice. Long time ago, when he was just starting out. Ferne was maybe fourteen, fifteen, but a woman, just the same. He squired her around a bit. But so did every other young buck in Omega."

"What about Jase Franklyn?"

Hendrycks looked surprised. His mouth hung open. "Jase? You broke it right there. Let's go back to town."

"I was just wondering," Barney said. "Don't get sore. Ferne seems to have known every important man in town. Why not Franklyn?"

"He's no man for the ladies, son. Forget it. I better start hunting up Ferne before Straehle get his paws on her and builds up a nice yarn about her and Charley."

Barney looked back at the quiet, silent bungalow. It seemed too quiet, too silent. "Perhaps she's inside and just doesn't want to let us in."

Hendrycks was startled again. "You get disturbing

ideas. First thing you know, you'll have me working overtime."

"The murderer may be working overtime, too," Barney said.

They went back to the house. The windows were all locked. Chief Hendrycks called the girl's name, and his voice went echoing away over the shadowy lake. There was no answer. Barney felt uneasy. Finally the chief took a long hunting knife and snicked open the catch on a screened door. They went through the house quickly, but Ferne was not there. The bottle of rye was empty. Barney went into the bedroom, opened dresser drawers upon mixed clothing, checked the closets, opened two suitcases, turned and saw the chief watching him.

"You still figure she heard about Alex and ran away?"

"No," Barney said. "She's somewhere around. Nothing seems to be missing."

"Just Alex Kane's crossbow," Hendrycks said quietly.

Barney stared. "Alex had one, too?"

"Brought it back with him from Korea. Reckon he got interested in them antique weapons because of Mal Hunter's collection. He showed it to Mal when he got back, and Mal offered him five hundred dollars for it, but he wouldn't sell it. Told everybody around town he would show Mal Hunter that some things couldn't be bought for any price. Some of us got a laugh out of it."

"How do you know it's missing?"

"While you were checking Ferne's clothes to see if she packed, I looked. It ain't here. Come on, we'll go back to town."

9

Barney returned to the Omega Hotel and spent twenty minutes packing, then showered and shaved and decided to have dinner where he was. He bought an Omega Times and read it while waiting to be served. It was a decorous and prim little newspaper, and the evening edition had only a small account of the finding of Alex Kane's body. And a careful perusal of the news story still left one in doubt whether the tragedy was murder or a simple drowning accident. Obviously, nothing was done to make any summer visitors feel uneasy. Barney put the newspaper away and concentrated on an excellent dinner.

He was on his second cup of coffee when the waitress came back and told him he was wanted on the phone. Barney followed her to a booth off the lobby and left the folding door open for what breeze came through the wide entrance to the veranda.

"Mr. Forbes?" a soft voice said. "This is Jason Franklyn."

"Speak of the devil," Barney said.

"I beg your pardon?"

"Nothing. I was just reading your interesting newspaper, and thinking a bit about you."

"I see. You understand, the Chamber of Commerce deplores any unfavorable publicity. However, I wish to apologize for any feeling of slight you may have about our meeting this morning."

"I hadn't thought much about it."

Franklyn's laugh was uneasy. "As a matter of fact, it is quite important that I see you again. Are you free this evening?"

"What's so important?"

"I would rather not mention it over the telephone. It is a small town, you know. Someone is here with me who finds it urgent to speak to you."

"At your house?"

"Yes. We are waiting."

"Who is it?"

"Come and see."

Barney hung up. He paid his dinner check, settled with the desk clerk for his room, and had an aged bell-hop carry his light bag to the rented car. It was dark when he turned into the road to Omega.

A narrow driveway made a dark slot between the press building and the ugly Victorian house in the rear, off the main square. There were no other cars parked in front of the old mansion. Lights glowed in the tall windows and touched the wide veranda steps where Barney had seen Branthorpe's two hoodlums waiting for him that morning. He let the car door slam and went up to ring the old brass pull-bell.

Ancient lace curtains that looked as if they had not been taken down for a decade obscured his view of the dim hallway beyond. He listened to frogs croaking in the swampy underbrush behind the house. There was only a faint murmur of traffic on the street beyond the dark bulk of the newspaper plant. He rang again.

In a moment Jason Franklyn opened the tall double doors. He wore a faded red velvet smoking jacket and Turkish red slippers and corduroy slacks the color of doeskin. His thin, esthetic face cracked with a smile. "Ah, Mr. Forbes. Come in, do come in."

The hallway smelled of mildew and must. A patina of gray dust overlay a bronze statue of Mercury holding an unshaded yellow bulb on the newel post of the stairway. Franklyn's slippered feet made pattering sounds on the tessellated floor, which must have been as cold as a morgue slab in the winter season. Huge sliding library doors opened into an octagonal room with a Vermont marble fireplace, more Victorian statuary, a serpentine-front china closet filled with Dresden pieces, all sentimental and sugary. A tall man stood waiting for them with his back to the fireplace, hands clasped behind him, shoulders bowed. His head was bald, his nose was long, his eyes deep-set and sharp in his gaunt face. He looked rather like a broken eagle.

It was Jan Hunter.

Franklyn's hands fluttered. "I hope you are not too surprised, Mr. Forbes. Jan and I are old friends. Jan arrived in Omega on the evening train and came straight here. No one knows he is in town, and he asks that we respect this confidence and keep his presence here to ourselves."

Barney smiled grimly. "It's just as well, perhaps. I was considering a trip to New York to see you again, Mr. Hunter."

Hunter cleared his throat. "Indeed?"

"And you know damned well why I wanted to see you."

"I beg your pardon?"

Franklyn said quickly. "A drink, gentlemen? Tea? I have some very fine imported—no? Perhaps some Benedictine that Mother preferred. There is still a bottle or two left."

"Sit down, Jase," Hunter said. "You make me nervous." He looked tweedy, in the town-and-country style promoted by expensive magazines, and he smelled of fine bourbon and Havana cigars. His figured necktie was a shade too youthful, as if his latent desire to play around town was exposed in this one selection and gave the show away. Otherwise he was the well-tailored clubman, with most of his forties behind him, but still virile enough. His sharp hawk's eyes fixed on Barney's tall figure. They were wounded eyes in which the predatory fires had been banked, but they still exhibited some of the command and power that existed as a family trait.

"I did not know about Alex Kane," he said to Barney, "when I started up here. Jase just told me. It is shocking, but not so shocking as it might have been had it come unexpectedly. You understand, of course, that something of this sort is exactly what I feared. This is precisely why I went to Peterman to ask for a reputable young man to—ah, investigate the matter and protect the family interests."

"Your interests, you mean," Barney said.

"Naturally, one thinks of oneself. But my brother—"

"You don't give a damn about your brother," Barney said. "Ever since he was old enough to count the value of a buck, he's taken over the family finances and dictated what you do and don't do, or else your tidy allowance and pension paid to you to keep you in New York would be cut off. I'm speaking bluntly," Barney said, his voice harsh, "because I'm a little disgusted by what I've discovered up here. I don't like being the cat's paw to pull your chestnuts out of the fire."

Jan Hunter stared blindly for a long, silent moment. Franklyn made a little sound of protest, then subsided. Hunter smiled, with no meaning behind it. "You are impertinent, Forbes."

"More than that," Barney said flatly. "I'm suspicious and insulting. You know a lot more about this affair up here than you intimated down in Peterman's office, when I was first retained. You implied that your concern was solely for Malcolm's welfare, and it didn't take long to learn that nobody in Omega has any doubt that Malcolm can take care of himself. I've been told from all

sides that your temerity in interfering in Malcolm's affairs is astonishing. It raises a rather curious question,
Mr. Hunter. What suddenly gave you the courage to send
me up here?"

Hunter exhaled slowly and sat down, bony legs folding
acutely at the joints. He leaned forward, hands clasped
between his knees, shoulders bowed. His bald head shone
in the light from a baroque fringed lamp on a massive
library table. He sighed again. Franklyn's sharp face
twitched.

"I think Malcolm is dead," Hunter said quietly.

"What makes you think so?"

"I have nothing to substantiate my feeling. I do not
think Malcolm killed Alex Kane. You see—I saw him that
night."

Barney heard Franklyn draw in a deep breath. He sat
still and waited.

"I was here in Omega the night my brother and Alex
Kane fought over that girl. I spoke to Mal not an hour
afterward. He was quite drunk, but there was no murder
in him. He said he planned to go away for a few weeks
and that was the last I heard of him."

"Did he say where he was going?"

"No."

"Then why did you call me into it?"

"I was uneasy. It is difficult to describe the intangible
feeling of disaster I had—and still have. I might as well
state frankly that I have no use for Evelyn, Mal's wife."
The eagle cracked his big, bony knuckles, looked up
sharply, then studied the faded oriental rug. "Nor have
I much use for Felix Branthorpe. I resent both of them.
My sister—she's in Paris—and I have suffered many in-
dignities at Malcolm's hands, and I feel that Evelyn and
Felix are at the bottom of it all."

"It couldn't just be Mal's nasty temperament, could it?"

"Mal is a strong and violent man. True. But not toward

me. Never toward me."

"But he paid you a regular pension to keep you away from here, didn't he?"

"Yes, he did."

"And you think you might lose some of your inheritance to Malcolm's wife, if something fishy is going on?"

"Precisely."

"That's your story," Barney said, "but I don't have to buy it. I think you screwed up your courage to send me here on only one basis. You not only *think* Malcolm is dead—you're sure of it."

Hunter's mouth opened like a trap and shut again.

"Please . . ." Franklyn murmured.

"Stay out of this, Jase," Hunter said. "Mr. Forbes is working for me. He is entitled to his thoughts, however much I may resent them." He stood up, unfolding angularly. He was a very tall, spare, loose-jointed man. "Mr. Forbes, I want you to find my brother—dead or alive. That is what I am paying you for. I will take the responsibility for anything Malcolm may do out of vindictive spite, if he is alive and resents my interference. But I must find him and I must learn the truth about Alex Kane's death. I beg you to spare no effort in doing so. And I must add that speed is of the essence."

"Why the rush?"

Hunter paced restlessly, cracking his knuckles again. His head thrust forward on his spare neck. "Last month, Malcolm cut off my income. I am rather deeply in debt. I must get some money at once."

"One way or the other, eh?" Barney asked. "Alive or dead."

"Exactly."

"And if I discover that *you* killed Malcolm?" Barney asked quietly.

Hunter's head came up. His eyes were stony. "No such contingency will arise."

"Are you apt to be suspected?"

"I may be. But I assure you, I've killed no one."

Barney sat down thoughtfully. He had the feeling he was trapped in a morass of hidden motivation, and his instincts made him rebel. He did not like it. For two cents, he would walk out on the problem at this moment, except for a nagging sense of conscience that would always pursue him, if he did. He recognized this fault in himself, this lack of objectivity where both Charley Danger was concerned—and the woman Evelyn Hunter. He remembered Evelyn Hunter's eyes—soft, wounded, betrayed. The feeling persisted that he might be on the wrong side of the fence insofar as his own ethics were concerned.

Finally he said: "You don't seem too worried about who murdered Alex Kane."

"If it was Malcolm, I want to know."

"And if he's alive, he'll resent your knowledge."

Hunter said: "Are you afraid of that?"

"No," Barney said. "Just respectful. And cautious."

"Malcolm is a dangerous man—if he is alive and if he is guilty. If you have any reservations—"

"You're not worried about Mal, are you?" Barney interrupted.

"No. But only because I think he is dead."

Franklyn said hesitantly: "Jan, you can't be sure. I don't know why you persist in such a belief. There is nothing to show that anyone killed Malcolm. He may be anywhere. Right here in town, perhaps. You know how he is. Don't you think a little caution might be wise?"

There was still a trace of steel in the gaunt man. Hunter's eyes flashed. "I'll make my own decisions. For too many years, I've been content to let Mal handle the finances, gather all the reins into his hands, controlling everything. I've had enough of it. I intend to make a fight of it." He swung to Barney. "Find him. Alive or dead, find him."

"And then?"

"Then I think that circumstances will dictate what to do next." Hunter's attitude became one of dismissal. "I shall remain here as Jason's guest for the next day or two. I'd appreciate it if you did not mention to anyone my presence in Omega, since I have no relish for police questioning. It is not that I have anything to hide. I simply prefer privacy. You may get in touch with me through Franklyn whenever you have anything to report."

"I'll do that," Barney said.

Frankyn saw him to the door and paused beside the bronze Mercury on the newel post. The naked light bulb was dusty. He spoke in a whisper, his hands fluttering again. "I wonder if you could advise me. I called Straehle, and received little satisfaction; but after all, it is a matter of news importance, you see. I understand that Ferne Kane is missing."

Barney kept his voice level. "Is she?"

"I thought you might know something about it."

"She isn't at her house," Barney said. "I went there with Hendrycks. How do you mean, missing?"

Franklyn's pale hands moved like ghosts in the dim light. "I understand she has not been found for questioning."

"How well do you know Ferne?" Barney asked.

Franklyn started to smile, then decided against it. "I suppose she has managed to interest many men in Omega."

"Including you?"

"A very attractive girl, in some respects."

"She's a tramp," Barney said flatly.

Nothing changed in Franklyn's eyes, except that something seemed to recede a little in his face. "Yes. A tramp. Of course."

"Good night to you," Barney said.

He went out through the double doorway, down the veranda steps, and across the weedy lawn to where he had left his car. Nobody jumped at him from the tangled brush. Nobody was waiting for him inside the dark coupe. He felt mildly surprised.

10

HE SPENT an hour trying to locate Chief Hendrycks and finally gave it up. He had no wish to see D.A. Straehle. He spent another forty minutes driving around the north end of the lake, pausing at Ferne Kane's place. It looked unchanged in the moonlight—empty and desolate. No lights shone in the windows. The screened door that Hendrycks had broken open was still unlocked. He drove away and considered stopping at the Hunter estate on the opposite shore, but by then it was ten o'clock and it had been a long day. Besides, there had been a message in Charley Danger's eyes when he tossed him the keys to his house, Barney remembered, and he turned into the road that led to Half Moon Cove.

The moonlight lay like quicksilver on the surface of the lake. Katydids shrilled in the treetops, heralding the autumn along with the chilly wind that came from the north. The cabin plane tugged uneasily at her moorings in the cove, and the rowboat bumped restlessly on the landing as Barney walked to the door of the redwood house perched on sturdy posts between the wooded mountainside and the shore. The shadows were sharp and black, moving with the movement of the trees in the cold wind.

Barney let himself into Danger's house at the upper level, where the living room windows faced the lake. The furniture in the room made angular patterns, all ebony and silver. There was the scent of cigarette smoke in the air, and perfume, and he paused with his hand groping for the light switch near the door.

"Please," Evelyn Hunter's voice came whispering out of the darkness. "The moonlight is enough."

He let his hand drop to his side and stood still.

"I'm over here," she added. "In the chair by the window."

He saw her then, in a deep wing-chair that faced the view of the lake. Only her face and the deep ivory cleft of her neckline were visible, floating among the shadows as if detached from reality. Then he saw that she wore dark velvet toreador slacks and ballet slippers and a thin cashmere sweater of black as well. With her dark hair, the effect was startling, as if her face were disembodied. His eyes shone white in the moonlight as he came around to face her.

"I've been waiting for you for two hours," she said quietly.

"I didn't see your car."

"I walked."

"It must be over four miles."

"I like to walk," she said.

"How did you get in?"

"I have a key," she said.

He had no comment on that. She turned her head toward him, and he saw that she sat with her legs tucked under her. Again his heart lurched, because she was so much like Lil, and yet she wasn't Lil and never could be. Her cigarette glowed and her eyes took on a luminosity from the red coal for an instant as her face emerged from the shadows and then retreated.

He sat down. "Did you come here alone?"

"Yes," she said simply. "I went to the courthouse and spoke to Charley. He told me you would be here tonight. He told me to help you in any way I can. Charley doesn't take to many men the way he's taken to you. He trusts you, even though he's only just met you."

"Does Felix know you are here?"

"No."

"He's quite a watchdog, isn't he?"

"He frightens me," the girl said. "There is something too intense about him. He always has a single purpose in mind. It's something he wants, and I don't know what it is. I used to think it was me, but I'm not sure now. It makes me nervous." She laughed softly. "It seems to me I spoke to you this way before."

"It's all right," he said. "I'm glad you're here. Can I fix you a drink?"

"I've already prepared some. You'll find them in the kitchen icebox. Please don't turn on the lights. You can find your way by moonlight."

Shrugging, he found the door he wanted and found the drinks she had mixed. She was at home here, knowing the intimacies of this house, comfortable in it, somehow suiting it. He shrugged again. It didn't have to mean anything. There was still a quick pulsing in him, because she reminded him so strongly of Lil, and for a moment he stood quietly in the darkness of the kitchen, the drinks in hand, while waves of deep anguish and longing shook him. He thought of what Chief Hendrycks had said, about his looking for something, and he wondered how Hendrycks had managed to strike so close to the truth. It reminded him not to underestimate the slow-spoken, friendly cop.

She had not moved when he returned with the cold drinks. Her eyes looked black, dreaming over the view of the lake. He could see much more clearly now. The room was warm and comfortable, logs had been set for a fire on the fieldstone hearth, the tiers of books looked friendly against the walls.

"I know you want to question me," she said. "Why

don't you begin. I wasn't completely honest with you earlier today."

"I want to know about Malcolm, your husband," he said. "I want to know if he's alive."

Her voice flattened, lost its richness. "Yes. He is."

He paused. "Have you heard from him?"

"Yes."

"When?"

"Several days—over a week ago."

"Do you know where he is?"

"I know where the telegram came from?"

"Telegram?"

Her eyebrows lifted. "Why are you so surprised?"

"I shouldn't be. Straehle, Hendrycks, Jase Franklyn, and everyone else in town seems so sure that Mal Hunter will come back. Small wonder they want to cover for him. I keep forgetting what a small town is like. Everybody of importance must know about that telegram."

She laughed softly. "It didn't say anything much. Just that he would be back soon. And to sign any checks that Felix wanted me to sign, in matters concerning the estate."

He breathed quietly. "Do you do that often?"

"Oh, yes."

"For large sums of money?"

"Some of them. Most are just petty cash."

"Any big ones since last week?"

"Two. Each one for over a hundred thousand dollars."

"Payable to whom?"

"A Chase National account in New York City."

"In Malcolm's name?"

"Oh, yes."

He tried his drink. There seemed to be no hurry. She had used quinine water with gin, and he was not particularly fond of it. "All right," he said. "Where is he?"

"Malcolm is in Canada," she said, and her voice continued on the same flat, dead level it maintained whenever she spoke of Malcolm Hunter. "At a place called Lake Quenniboscet. He has a lodge up there that he uses for hunting and fishing, every now and then. I've only been there once. I didn't like it. It's a bit too remote from civilization to suit me."

"You said you spoke to Mal the night he fought with Alex Kane. Do you think he killed Alex? Was he worried, upset, frightened?"

"He was drunk," she said simply. "He could have been in any state of mind at all, and it might have been meaningless. He often has nightmares—I don't know what they're about. I couldn't say how he was."

"Did he take the plane alone?"

"No. Al Greeley was with him."

"Greeley is the pilot who took over Charley's job?"

"Yes."

"You saw this Greeley yourself? You watched them take off?"

She was silent for so long he thought she had forgotten his question. Moonlight silvered on the glass in her hand. Looking at her, Barney was surprised by a sudden twist of desire that went through him.

"I'm not sure," she said thoughtfully. She frowned, touched the tip of a finger to her cheek. "I saw someone down on the float who I assumed was Al. He got into the plane with Malcolm, I'm sure of that. I simply assumed it was Malcolm's pilot."

"But Mal could fly himself, couldn't he?"

"Oh, yes."

"Do you know where I could find this Greeley fellow?"

"He lives in the town of Jackson. Anyone could tell you the address. I suppose I have it somewhere in the house. But he must be up in Canada with Malcolm now." She leaned forward. "I hope you believe me,

Barney. I don't know why Jan hired you, but I'm glad you're here. Someone must look into what happened to Alex—someone who isn't involved with this town or the people in it. Someone with courage. Charley has that courage, but Charley couldn't be objective—"

She broke off. He was not listening to her. From down below came the soft creak of a door being opened.

Evelyn's eyes went wide and luminous as Barney stood up. He moved in absolute silence, swiftly, like a drifting shadow. At the head of the stairs to the gallery below, he paused and looked back. The girl was only visible as a lovely, detached face against the velvet shadows surrounding her.

Someone moved across the lower floor, paused, took two more steps, paused again. Metal made a soft clinking sound. Then there came the smooth, oiled click of a gun being cocked.

Barney flattened against the wall in the shadows. He listened to a deep pulsing, night silence that was not silence at all, but a low murmuring of the wind in the brush, the tapping of a branch against an upper window, the lapping of tiny wavelets on the pebbly lake shore.

Nothing else.

He waited. He thought of the lights having been out in the house, and wondered if the intruder expected to find the place empty. But his car was out there in plain sight. The intruder hoped he was asleep, then. Gently, easily, he worked his gun from his pocket and faced the darkly yawning stairwell. He did not look back at Evelyn Hunter again.

Without warning, a blinding light burst in his eyes.

He jumped, diving instantly into the white wall below. There came a sudden yell of surprise, the thunderous burst of a gun going off, and then he slammed into someone standing at the foot of the stairs. They both went crashing down. The flashlight in the other's hand went spinning away across the floor and shattered and went out. Fingers clawed at his face. He felt the strength of the other man as something incredibly hard and steely. Pain gripped his throat and he pulled back, struck with the gun, and missed as the other squirmed away with the speed of a cat. As Barney lunged after him, he heard footsteps going away, quick and smooth. A door slammed. He felt a rush of clear, cold air and ran in pursuit.

Moonlight glittered on the cove, turned the trees to black and silver, etched sharp shadows on the road. The katydids sang their pulsating song. Barney took a few steps toward his car and paused.

Nothing.

Nobody.

The gun felt warm and slippery in his hand. He watched the shadows move in the wind, studied the waters of the cove, looked up the road. Whoever the man had been, he was gone, melting into the night woods with the smooth sinuosity of a savage.

"Barney?"

It was Evelyn, behind him.

"Keep your voice down," he whispered.

"Are you all right?"

"Yes. What's the matter?"

"Who was it? Did you see?"

"No."

"I saw him from the window," she said. "It was Felix."

"Why would he come sneaking in here?"

She shuddered, standing beside him. "He follows me. He follows me everywhere. He watches over me the same way he watches over the rest of Malcolm's goods and chattels. I'm Malcolm's property, and Felix is loyal to Malcolm." Her teeth chattered.

"Take it easy," he said.

"I can't help it. I feel sick."

"Did he ever follow you here before?"

"No. Not that I know of."

He put his arm around her and felt the deep, wracking shudders that tortured her body. Without pretense, she leaned against him, her arms clinging about his neck, drawing his face down to hers, pressing her against him almost with a frenzy of fear. Her shuddering did not stop.

"Inside," he said. "You need a drink."

"I'm—I'm so afraid."

"He's gone. There's nothing to be afraid of."

"He'll tell Malcolm."

"I'll explain everything," Barney said.

"You'll never get a chance. Mal will kill you."

"Come inside," Barney said. "I'll build the drinks this time."

He disengaged her gently. Her head was lowered as he led her like a child back upstairs to the living room. But she was not a child. He was only too well aware of this. He led her to the chair she had occupied when he first arrived, told her to stay there, and made a quick round of the house, checking all doors and windows to be certain they were locked. He returned to the living room and she stood up to come to him. Her eyes were great dark pools of moving shadow. She looked slender and womanly and beautiful, and he felt something intangible tremble between them.

"I don't want a drink, Barney," she whispered. "I don't want to leave here. I can't go back to that house now."

"You must, Evelyn."

"I want you," she said with soft directness. "I need you. Help me. You need me, too. You know you do."

Lil, he thought.

Her mouth was soft and yielding when he kissed her. For an instant he felt weighted by an intolerable sense of guilt. He felt her lips move under his as she spoke.

"You don't love me," she whispered. "I understand all that." The weight of her body pulled him down. "For you, I can only be a substitute for the one you lost."

He was silent.

He looked down at her, saw that her eyes were wide, watching him.

"And I don't love you," she said quietly.

"Then who am I substituting for?" he asked.

"Does it matter?"

"It might matter a lot."

"No. You and I need each other. For tonight, anyway. It will be enough. Why question the need we have?"

He saw the shine of silent tears on her soft face. In the moonlight and the stillness, her features blurred and blended with the face he carried in his memory, and as he bent toward her again, he felt something rip and tear inside him and there was a deep, wild flood of needing and wanting in him that drew him to her with irresistible force. . . .

11

HE DREAMED of Lily again.

Dreaming, he groaned in his sleep and heard the sound of his voice crying out, harsh and strong against the silence of the night. The dream was a bad one, the worst he had ever had, seeing her again the way she looked when the ambulance delivered her to the hospital, after the accident that killed her. Every ugly, horrible detail was lived again, every incredible moment of not accepting, denying, refusing the knowledge that she no longer lived.

Dreaming, he heard the sound of the wind, the tapping of a branch on the window, the purling of the lake on the shore—and of someone entering the house again.

Barney awoke.

He lay still, sprawled, motionless, hearing the echo of his nightmare fade away. His heart still pounded and his eyes focused on the pattern of the window frame, the dim luminosity of the night beyond. Sweat covered him. He moved his right hand slowly and carefully, searching for Evelyn. Nothing. The couch was still warm where she had slept, her pillow still indented by her head; her fragrance still lingered subtly in the air.

She was gone.

He had the feeling that several hours had passed and when he sat up and looked at his watch, he saw it was four o'clock in the morning. The moon had set, and a deep darkness covered the lake beyond the windows.

He shivered in the chill air as the sweat dried on him.

He started to call Evelyn's name, then was silent as he heard the sound from downstairs again. It was a heavy tread, cautious and yet firm, as if the owner knew where he was going. A man. Not Evelyn. Felix Branthorpe again? He reached for his gun.

"Barney?"

The voice drifted up to him on the dark, cool air.

He was awake all at once, his sleep and his nightmare gone.

"Here," he said.

It was Charley Danger.

The Indian stood at the foot of the stairs, dimly out-lined against the tall windows below the gallery. Water streamed from him, puddling darkly on the tiled floor. He was naked to the waist, and his dark hair hung in wet loops over his flat brow. His eyes were twin white cres-cents, looking up.

"Put down your gun, Barney," he said softly. "It's quite all right."

Barney went downstairs. "How did you get here? How did you get out of Straehle's coop?"

"I broke out. It was easy enough. I didn't hurt any-body. They don't even know I'm gone yet, but just to be on the safe side, I avoided the roads and swam across the lake. The water is damned cold."

"Why did you do it? They'll jail you for sure, now."

The Indian smiled bleakly. "The way Straehle is turn-ing himself inside out to cover for Malcolm Hunter, I didn't stand a chance, anyway. I'm glad you came here. I need help."

"You've got it, of course," Barney said. "But I don't see what you can do. In Straehle's eyes, you've convicted yourself by breaking out."

Danger made a chopping gesture with his strong brown hand. "Have you talked to Evelyn yet?"

"She was here," Barney said quietly. "She just left."

Danger looked at him in silence. Something changed in his lean face, but the shadows were too deep for Barney to be sure what it was. Then the other man said: "Evelyn is a wonderful girl."

"I think she's in love with you," Barney said slowly.

Danger seemed taller, darker, in the shadowed room. He exhaled softly in unmistakable relief. "Don't jump at conclusions, man. We've got to find Malcolm Hunter."

"I know where he is," Barney said. He told the Indian what Evelyn Hunter had told him about the lodge up in Canada. "Does Mal know how you feel about his wife?"

"Evelyn isn't his wife. Not really. Oh, they're legally married, and all that. But she doesn't belong to him. He regards her as property, as an ornament to his way of living, that's all. The sadistic bastard has no thought for her real feelings." Danger's voice shook, then steadied, grew calm and decisive. "It's a three-hour flight up there. We'll skip getting clearance for it, naturally. There's gas in the plane—I topped the tanks myself, yesterday morning. We could make it by dawn."

Barney was wide awake now. "Is that why you broke out—to hunt for Mal?"

"To hunt for the man who killed Alex," the Indian said softly. "Or the woman." There was hard steel in his voice, a grim and inflexible purpose in his lean face. "You don't have to come with me if you don't want to. You'll be compounding a felony or something, assisting my jailbreak, if you do."

"Change your clothes," Barney said. "I'll fix a thermos of coffee."

"Ten minutes," Danger said.

They shook hands on it.

Upstairs, Barney swiftly put the couch together, found a sweater that fitted him, and went down to the kitchen to make coffee. He used lights wherever he went, and he was just pouring a thermos jug full when the telephone rang in the next room. He had been thinking of Evelyn, uneasy about her disappearance, and he was relieved when he heard her voice.

"Barney?"

"Here," he said. "Where are you?"

"I walked home. I thought you were asleep."

"I was. Are you all right?"

"Yes. I saw Felix. He didn't say anything to me. I'm better now. You don't have to worry about me. I just want to thank you," she said in a low voice. "For understanding everything. I'm sorry things couldn't—be otherwise."

"So am I," he said quietly. It was strange, the slow, rising sense of relief and freedom he gained from her words. It was as if a nightmare had been dispelled, a weight lifted from his back. "You've done a lot for me."

"I'm glad."

"I think you ought to know," he said, "that Charley is here."

She gasped. "Oh, no!"

"He's all right. Don't worry about him."

"Please! Let me speak to him."

Barney turned and saw the Indian behind him. He handed the phone in silence to Danger and went out. For a moment or two he heard the murmur of Danger's voice, speaking swiftly and with soft urgency. He went downstairs then and out on the float to the moored cabin plane that rocked gently in the pre-dawn breeze. The air felt fresh and clear. His mind was alert and buoyant with a freedom he had almost forgotten.

Danger joined him in a moment, quick and efficient. "Let's go."

The cough and sputter of the motors awakened loud echoes that reverberated back and forth from the steep mountain slopes across the dark lake. There was only the luminous starshine to guide their slow taxiing trip out of the cove. Here and there across the lake a light went on in a summer cottage as the residents were aroused by the racket. The motors settled down to a smooth roar in a matter of minutes. Barney wondered if Straehle would hear the sound and interpret it correctly enough to check on the courthouse cell where Charley Danger was supposed to be. Tension built up in him as Danger bent forward over the controls and revved up the twin motors. The plane gathered speed, hurtling across the dark surface of the lake. Beyond the perimeter of the instrument panel, there was nothing to see except the dual white knives of spray from the pontoons. The plane lifted, settled, and lifted again, rising smoothly. A wall of dark trees loomed ahead, wavered, then sank below.

Barney exhaled with relief. Danger grinned.

"I could take off blindfolded from this lake," Danger said. "There was nothing to worry about."

"What about Lake Quenniboscet?"

"It will be daylight when we get there—almost, anyway. I've been there before."

The plane was comfortably furnished, equipped with four seats and a luggage compartment, a small built-in bar, and gun-racks in the overhead that were empty now. Barney settled back in silence to let the time go by. His thoughts kept circling around Charles Danger and Evelyn Hunter, and his own affair with her tonight. He felt no sense of guilt about what had happened, but he wondered how the Indian would take it if or when he learned about it. Lil came into his thoughts, but with a softness and ease that had never been in him since the senseless accident that took her life. Evelyn had known what he needed and had given him a small part of herself to banish the ghost that haunted him. He wondered

if the cure would be effective. He had helped her, too,
in her loneliness and terror. Their mutual instincts had
left nothing to regret.

There was a grayness in the eastern sky when they
crossed the St. Lawrence and continued north. The
world below was still shrouded in night, however, when
Charley grunted and put the plane in a wide, circling
maneuver. Looking down from their altitude of three
thousand feet, Barney could make out only a featureless
murk, composed of looming hills and twisting streams
that gleamed faintly through tall, virgin evergreen for-
ests. No lights shone down there.

"We were lucky," Danger said. "The Air Force radar
and C.D. spotters didn't nick us. This is it. Hang on."

"Any other cabins on the lake?"

"No. Hunter owns it all."

The plane dropped smoothly down. Dark clumps of
trees, the sudden sheer wall of a granite cliff, the flickering of water passed under the pontoons. It was darker
on the surface than Barney had expected. The roar of the
motors abruptly eased as Danger throttled down. An
opaqueness appeared beyond the plexiglass windshield, a
dark expanse, narrow and twisting, that was Lake Quenniboscet. There came a jolt as the pontoons touched
down, another jolt, and water sprayed on either side of
the cabin. Barney felt himself thrust forward in his
seat by the deceleration. Then Danger suddenly grunted
and the plane slewed crazily to port. Barney glimpsed a
looming white object in the water ahead, then a wing-tip
kissed the surface of the lake and the plane slewed again,
and something snapped with a quick, brittle sound.
Water struck the cabin window like a hammer blow.
Barney's head slammed against something and he heard
Danger's curse. There came a stunning shock as the

plane came to a rocking halt.

Silence folded in.

They were still afloat, but the plane was canted slightly to port. Danger cut off the ignition and the props were motionless. Barney blew out a deep breath.

"What is it?"

"Obstruction in the channel. Wasn't there before."

"Are we all right?"

"I'll check the damage soon as it's light." There was a cut on the Indian's jaw, and blood trickled darkly from it. His face was grim. "Look behind you. It's Mal Hunter's plane."

Barney climbed out and stood on the pontoon. The air was cold, and in the murky dawn he could see they had come to a halt only a few lengths from a long, narrow dock that extended from the wooded shore. A neat low modern hunting lodge with an immense stone chimney stood against a background of dense woods. A chill wind blew against his back from the lake. Turning, he saw the white object he had glimpsed just before they halted. It was the tail of a plane, originally white, but blackened and twisted now by smoke, the aluminum skin torn, one tail flap wrenched completely away. The depth of the lake could not have been more than ten feet at that point.

"You're sure it's Hunter's plane?"

Danger joined him on the pontoon. "There's no mistake. And there's no one in the lodge, either, or they'd have lights on to greet us. We'll let the wind blow us in to the landing."

The building on shore remained shrouded in darkness. Their plane rocked easily, swinging in the wind, and the gap to the wooden dock closed rapidly. Barney leaped ashore, caught the line Danger tossed to him, and made the plane fast. The Indian joined him, turning to stare at the wreckage protruding from the surface of the lake.

"Come on. We'll see what happened."

"How far are we from the nearest telephone?" Barney asked.

"Almost sixty miles."

"Any roads in?"

"Only a canoe route the local people use. But there should be a caretaker around here. Henry George." Danger frowned and touched the cut on his jaw thoughtfully. His eyes were brooding as he stared at the lodge. "This was Mal's hideout. Nobody knew about it but myself and a few of his chosen friends. I never mentioned it to Evelyn, but she learned about it, somehow. There were some pretty wild nights spent up here. I guess that's all over now."

"We don't know that Mal is dead. He sent Evelyn that telegram. How would he have done it from here?"

"I don't know." Danger shrugged. "But if anyone was in that plane when it blew up, he's dead."

They walked up to the lodge. The light was brightening at last, and the woods behind the house was alive with the songs of birds and the high chattering of squirrels. A doe stared calmly at them from the very edge of the clearing, then suddenly took fright and bounded away, white tail flickering for an instant before it was gone.

"Mal always had everything either flown in or carried by portage to Quenniboscet," Danger said. "There's a diesel plant for power, a deep freeze, all the comforts of home. You can hear the diesel running now."

"Then somebody must still be around."

"Maybe."

The house echoed emptily when they went in through the unlocked front door. The main room was enormous, stretching the length of the structure, with a kitchen and storerooms in the back and bedrooms above, beyond a high gallery with clerestory windows. Trophies of the hunt were displayed everywhere. Danger moved quickly ahead, throwing open the doors to the various rooms, checking the diesel shed behind the house. Only one of the bedrooms showed any sign of recent use—in the form of a blue canvas airplane bag with the initials *M.H.* stamped on it. Barney zipped it open and checked a compact wardrobe of hunting togs. The rest of the house was clean and spotless, except for an accumulation of cold ashes on the big stone hearth.

"Nobody," Danger muttered.

It was light enough now for them to see the wreckage of the other plane clearly. Several canoes and a speedboat were tied up at the dock, with canvas raincovers buttoned down securely. They were standing on the dock examining the boats when a hail came from across the water and Barney saw a light canoe coming toward them.

An old man with a huge white mustache, startling against his nut-brown face, was in the canoe.

"That's Henry George," Danger murmured.

In a matter of only a minute the canoe reached the dock and the old man climbed out. He wore a checked flannel shirt against the bite of the wind and high leather boots over tucked-in khaki pants. He spoke to Danger in quick French patois that Barney could not understand. Danger asked sharp questions, pointing to the wrecked plane. Another spate of voluble explanation followed. Barney could only wait. There was nothing to be read from the old man's weathered, wrinkled face. Finally Henry George turned and they started walking along the lake shore, away from the lodge.

"Henry wasn't here when the plane arrived," Danger said. "All he knows is that he heard the explosion and saw a burst of flame from about five miles away. By the time he got here, it was all over. He figures the plane must have struck a snag as it came in for a landing and dived under. The gas tanks went and that was it. We know Hunter was drunk enough the night he flew up here."

"But he didn't fly alone," Barney said.

"I know. Al Greeley was with him."

"Or somebody Evelyn thought was Al Greeley."

Danger looked at him. "I don't follow that one."

"She never saw the other man's face. Until we find Al Greeley, let's keep it open."

"You won't have far to go to find that hot-shot so-and-so. Henry fished him out of the plane wreck and buried him."

They had paused at a small clearing a hundred yards in from the lake shore. The old man said something to Danger, and pointed to a neat mound with a carefully shaped and painted white cross at the head of it. Danger's stare was level and sombre as they walked toward the grave. The corners of his mouth were tight and white as he spoke again.

"Henry says there wasn't much left of the body. The explosion and fire did a pretty complete job before the plane sank."

"Then how does Henry know it's Al Greeley?"

"He just says so."

"Did Henry ever see Greeley? Up until two weeks ago, you were Hunter's pilot. Did Greeley ever fly up here?"

Danger stared away at a robin perched atop a blasted pine nearby. The robin was singing in full throat at the rising sun. A mist came up over the lake and moved idly in the light, chill wind.

"You have a thought there," he said quietly.

"Try another for size. Did Henry see Malcolm Hunter *after* the accident?"

There was more talk in French patois. The old man gestured volubly, then smoothed his huge white moustache. His small eyes looked angrily at Barney.

"Henry says Hunter was in the house when he got here. Locked himself up in it and yelled at him from out of the upper-floor window. Tossed a note down, which was the telegram Evelyn received. Henry tried to talk to him to find out what happened and to make sure that Hunter was all right, but he says Hunter was drunk —very, very drunk. So he took his canoe and paddled sixty miles to St. Joseph, the nearest telegraph office."

"Do you buy it?" Barney asked.

"I don't know."

"Ask Henry if Hunter was here when he came back."

"He wasn't."

"Then how did he get out of the woods? Where is he?"

Danger looked angry. "You seem to have all the ideas. You tell me."

"My guess," Barney said, "is that this is Hunter's grave. It was Hunter that Henry pulled out of the plane and buried."

"Then who was the other man?" Danger snapped. "It couldn't be Al Greeley. You don't know Al. A rumdum, with all his brains in his pants. A hot-shot flyer, but reckless. Buzzes golf courses, stunts, drinks too much, runs around. Not clever. An ape. A hired chauffeur."

"We'll have to find him."

"In these woods?" Danger asked. He waved a hand. "Look for a needle in a haystack. It will be easier."

"Maybe Al isn't in the woods," Barney said. "Maybe he never came up here at all. I'm not implying that Evelyn lied when she said she saw Greeley take off with Hunter. But she couldn't swear who it was. Yet the man who flew up here with Hunter—assuming I'm right and that Hunter is in this grave—flew up here for one purpose only. The plane could have been blown up deliberately, couldn't it, rather than be destroyed as an accident?"

"Yes," Danger said, biting at the word.

"Are any boats missing?"

"What?"

"Boats. Or other means of transportation. The second man, whether it's Hunter or someone else, had to get away from here and return to where he's usually seen. And he had to do it fast."

"It isn't possible. You don't realize how far we are from public transportation. It would take a week of walking—if you knew your way through the woods and didn't get killed or get lost and starve to death."

"Nevertheless, he did it," Barney said stubbornly.

"Or else Hunter is out there in the woods laughing at us right now." Danger paused. "Who would the other man be?"

"The man you're looking for," Barney said. "The man who killed Alex Kane."

12

It was late afternoon when they returned. They landed on a small lake five miles from the town of Jackson, twenty from Omega, and nobody seemed too alarmed or interested when Charley Danger rented a mooring for his plane at a public landing. They took a bus into Jackson and ate at the terminal. Danger was an easy, comfortable man to be with. He had the quiet grace and wariness of a woodland animal, and a high level of intelligence blended with a gentle humor. His tension was buried deep inside him, and he seemed at ease, without worry about the police search for him.

Together, they went looking for Al Greeley.

Jackson was a small crossroad town, not a resort at all, but a farm center. Except for the majestic mountain scenery, it could have been any of hundreds of similar towns scattered throughout the state. Al Greeley lived in a rooming house two blocks from the main street. It was a shabby, rundown clapboard house with a scrubby yard and sleazy curtains on the windows.

"I'll take it from here," Barney said. "The less anyone sees you, the better."

Danger nodded. Barney went ahead and rang the bell. It took a long time for the landlady to appear. She was a hard-bitten, dour woman with suspicious eyes that faded away into blank, marbly blue when Barney asked for Al Greeley.

"Not here," she snapped. "And if you're around to

collect on a bill, you're too late. He's had his spree and he's broke."

"When do you expect him back?"

"Never, I hope." She started to close the door and looked beyond him to Charley Danger, who lounged against the sagging picket fence. Her mouth opened, closed, opened again. She wiped her hands on her apron. "It's about a bill, isn't it?" she asked.

"Just the opposite," Barney said. "I owe Al some money and I thought I'd drop around to pay off. We had a little poker game the other night, but I haven't seen him since. He isn't away on a trip, is he?"

"Can't say. He comes and goes. Drunk most of the time, ugly when he's sober, mean when he's not." Something glistened in her shrewd eyes. "How much do you owe him?"

"Twenty dollars."

"He's behind in his rent for thirty-two. You could pay me, mister. I'll see him and tell him that you were here."

"I couldn't do that," Barney said. "Didn't he sleep here last night?"

"I never go into his room. He keeps it locked and cleans it himself." She sniffed. "If he cleans at all. Probably like a pigsty. Truth to tell, I'm kind of afraid of him, mean the way he is. I don't like to interfere with his coming and going, but if you see him today, you tell him I got to get my money or go to the police." She looked at Danger again, then up and down the street. Barney looked, too. It was just a street, hot and dusty in the late evening light. "Is that where Al got all that money lately? In your poker game?"

"When was this?"

Her eyes were like stones again. "For a pal of his, you don't know much about him, do you?"

Barney flattened his voice. "I'm not a pal."

She grunted with satisfaction. "Are you a cop?"

"In a way."

"You almost fooled me, mister." Again her eyes glistened. "I'll help you all I can. I hate that boozing ape. He's got me scared to death most of the time, bullying and yelling and drinking around. It's got so bad I can't let him stay and I'm afraid to ask him to git. I hope he's in bad trouble, this time. I hope it's for good." She paused. "Who's your friend out there?"

"Nobody. Maybe we can talk better inside."

"I'm busy. My time is valuable," she said.

"I'll pay you for it."

It cost him several bills from his wallet before she unlocked the door to Al Greeley's room. She hung back a little in the dim brown hallway, as if unsure of what might happen when he went in. He closed the door against her sharply inquisitive face.

It was just a room. A back window looked out upon a fenced yard, a side window faced the curtained windows of the house next door. Barney pinched the bridge of his nose, blew out his breath, and began a quick and methodical search. There was an iron bedstead, a Boston rocker, a steel foot-locker from Army days. The locker was fastened with a padlock that would have taken a hammer to smash. He didn't have a hammer. In the closet, he found a man's clothes, large size, mostly sport jackets and slacks, white shoes, heavy work shoes, a pile of old shirts pushed into a corner. On the dresser were military brushes, and on the brushes was a thin layer of gray dust. Stuck into the mirror frame above the dresser were snapshots of a number of different women in a number of exotic poses, all nude. In the wastebasket were four empty bottles of wine, two of cheap rye, and one of domestic champagne.

The bed had not been made, and it had a seedy, deserted look, as if it had not been slept in for some time. The air in the room was stale, smelling of sweat,

stagnant cigarette smoke, the dregs of the wine bottles.
Barney closed the closet door, tried another door, and
looked into a narrow bathroom with painted yellow walls
and an old iron tub with rusted fixtures. There was no
window, but a skylight operated by a long chain let
light and air inside. Around the tub, more pictures of
nude women were blatantly taped to the yellow wall.

The skylight was open. Barney stood on the edge of
the tub, reached up, and hooked his hands on the metal
frame overhead, then hauled himself up. There was a
small wooden platform without a railing, and the brick
house chimney. No bodies, no secret doors, nothing.

But something troubled him.

He lowered himself, stood still, frowned, and returned
to the bedroom to go through the dresser drawers. There
was a leather holster made to fit an Army .45 Colt, and
there was fresh oil in the holster. But no gun. There was
a framed picture of a man he assumed to be Al Greeley,
thrust under several laundered blue denim work shirts.
A bull of a man in an Air Force uniform, smiling into
the sun with the hangar of some faraway airfield in the
background. Small eyes close together, a hairline moustache, a big jaw that looked as if it might be glass. A
hard face, the face of a drinker, already showing signs
of bloat and sagging although the picture might have
been taken five years ago.

He was still troubled.

All at once he went back to the bathroom and looked
closely at the photographs taped to the wall over the
tub. Most of them were regular-sized snapshots, all were
lewd, all of different women of various ages, sizes and
shapes. There was a row of six of them, and above that
was a glossy enlargement of what must have been the
latest addition to the erotic gallery.

This photograph had a different quality than the
others. Instead of a cheap bedroom background, this

one had been taken out of doors, against a woodsy hillside. The girl leaned back against a large oak on the edge of a clearing, and the corner of a white bungalow was visible in one edge of the picture. The girl was different from the others, too. Younger, smiling, almost inviting despite the blatantly provocative, vulgar pose.

It was Ferne Kane.

Barney gave a soft, soundless whistle. His face was grim. He picked the tape loose, removing the photograph from the wall, and folded it once to put it into his pocket. Going out, he thumbed the catch on the door and locked it quietly behind him.

The landlady paused with one foot going down the steps. She looked back and waited for him.

"You seen it all?" she grated. There were two red spots on her gaunt cheeks that might have been embarrassment or dull anger. "Now you know why I don't go into his room. He ought to be arrested."

"I think he will be," Barney said.

"Can you tell me what he's done? I'd sure like to know. It might make me sleep better tonight, knowing the cops are after him."

"There's nothing for you to worry about. But if Al comes back, he might not like my being in his room. Suppose you give me a ring if he shows up." He told her Jason Franklyn's name in Omega. "I don't live there, but whoever answers will know where to get in touch with me. Don't tell them why you're calling. Just leave your name."

She was reluctant about it. "I'll see. I don't promise anything." She opened the front door for him and peered out at the street. "Looks like your friend couldn't wait."

Barney looked up and down the sidewalk.

Charley Danger was gone.

13

THERE was a bus from Jackson to Omega that let him off at the courthouse square at seven o'clock. He bought an Omega Times from the newsboy feeding the pigeons in the evening light and scanned it quickly. Jason Franklyn handled his news at a cool distance. There were no shrieking headlines about Charley Danger's jailbreak. Like the story of Alex Kane's death, the ambiguity of the story left one in doubt as to exactly what had happened. The only clear statement in the tersely worded story was that Charles Danger was being "sought" for questioning by District Attorney Hiram Straehle. No connection was made with Kane's death. Barney remembered that Chief Hendrycks had expected fireworks to further Straehle's political ambitions, and he wondered what had put the lid on the story insofar as Straehle was concerned. He walked into the Omega Times office.

The prim, gray woman clerk behind her railing looked no different than the first time Barney had seen her. She told him that Franklyn was not in the office, but at home.

"I'm glad he's not traveling again," Barney ventured.

Nothing changed in her face except for a slight arching of fine, intellectual brows. "Traveling?"

"As he was two weeks ago."

"You must be mistaken. Mr. Jason hasn't been out of Omega for ten years. It is something he takes pride in. His interests are entirely contained within our town, Mr. Forbes. His historical research, he often says, has convinced him that there is nothing to be seen or found elsewhere in the world beyond the limits of our town.

Omega is the world, and the world is Omega, he often says."

"Or the end of it," Barney suggested.

"Your irony is wasted upon me, Mr. Forbes. I agree entirely with Mr. Jason."

Her head moved in a gesture of dismissal. Her typewriter clacked busily. From down in the basement came the rumble of the presses and the sound of men's voices. There was a neat little brass sign upon her receptionist's desk. K. A. Franklyn. She didn't look like a sister. She couldn't be his wife. He gave up thinking about it and walked through the building and out the back door to the Victorian house in the rear.

It was unchanged. The yellow electric bulb still shone in the uplifted hand of Mercury, a-perch the newel post. Jason Franklyn still wore the Turkish slippers and silk smoking jacket. The dust on the mildewed draperies had gained a day's thickness, that was all. But when Franklyn opened the door for him, the editor's jaw pushed out and down and astonishment shone in his eyes.

"My word! Mr. Forbes, where have you been? Come in, come in! Don't you know the police are looking for you?"

"Why?" Barney asked blandly.

"Why? Because of Charles Danger, that's why! My word, we've been wondering all day what had happened to you! Do come in!"

In the hexagonal library room there was a small fire on the Vermont marble hearth, its warmth welcome against the chill of early autumn. Jan Hunter stood with his back to the flames as if he had not moved in twenty-four hours. But this time there was another man, rising swiftly from an English club chair, hands clenched into angry fists, face scowling at Barney's entrance. It was Felix Branthorpe.

"Well, well. Your man has made an appearance, Jan," Felix said in a hostile voice.

Jan Hunter bent his sad, eagle's face toward the estate manager. "Contain yourself, Felix. I'm sure Mr. Forbes has an explanation of why he helped Charles Danger escape from jail."

"I didn't help him," Barney said. "He did it alone. From what I've seen of him, there isn't much he couldn't do alone."

"Then you have seen him, have you not?" Hunter demanded.

"I've been with him all day," Barney admitted.

"Aiding and abetting a fugitive to escape," Branthorpe snapped. "Straehle will like that."

"I don't care what Straehle likes or dislikes," Barney said quietly. "I've had an interesting day with Danger. We flew up to Canada, and a number of questions have been raised as a result of the trip." He nodded toward Branthorpe's squat, powerful figure. "I'm glad you're here, Felix. You can answer some of the questions, without the help of your two muscle men. By the way, what happened to them?"

"I don't know anything about them," Branthorpe snapped. His dark eyes were sullen. A nerve jumped and twitched in his jaw. "Any muscle work that's needed, I can take care of myself. As you ought to know from last night."

Barney let the remark drop where it was. He swung abruptly to Jan Hunter. "Where did you go that Tuesday night when your brother and Alex Kane had their fight?"

"Straight back to New York," Hunter said. "Why?"

"You didn't fly to Canada with Malcolm?"

"I checked in at my club at nine o'clock on Wednesday morning. I went there straight from Grand Central."

"I suppose you can prove it?"

"Certainly." Hunter's sharp, hawk's face looked white

and pinched. "Did you find Malcolm up in Canada?"

Barney ignored the question, eyeing Jason Franklyn. "What about you, Mr. Franklyn? Did you leave Omega that night?"

Franklyn was unperturbed. His voice was mild, his smile patronizing. "I was right here in this house, working on my historical research. As a matter of fact, I never left the house for two days, I became so engrossed in some records on a General Ivory Pelham, a little-known Indian fighter who carried on a harassing campaign against Braddock—"

"I suppose you can prove you were here?"

"Naturally. But why should I?"

Barney swung again. "And you, Felix?"

"To hell with you," Branthorpe said. "I don't have to answer any of your questions. What are you trying to prove, anyway? The whole thing is clear now. Charley Danger took advantage of Mal's fight with Alex Kane to knock off Alex so he could play around with Ferne again. He made it look as if Mal did it, swiping a crossbow and putting it back in the house before it was missed. He knew his way around the house; he worked there long enough. He did it to have Ferne for himself."

Barney met the man's gaze with level eyes. "You know he isn't interested in Ferne any more."

Branthorpe flushed, bit his lip, and shrugged. "Then why did he break out of jail?"

"To get the man who killed Alex Kane. And he's apt to do it, too." Barney shrugged, and asked, "Has Ferne Kane shown up yet?"

Franklyn answered. "No. She has utterly disappeared."

"Has Hendrycks found Alex Kane's Korean crossbow?"

"That has vanished, too."

"May I ask," said Jan Hunter solemnly, "why you question us about our whereabouts two weeks ago?"

"It's very simple," Barney told him. A log cracked and

snapped in the fireplace, and a spark flew out onto the
faded oriental rug. Jason Franklyn meticulously put it
out. "Somebody flew up to Lake Quenniboscet with Malcolm Hunter that night. It was somebody who knew
about Hunter's yen for Ferne and who knew about
Malcolm's fight with Alex only a few hours before. Whoever it was, he killed Alex and made it look as if Malcolm was guilty, and managed to rattle Malcolm into
a quick flight north until the affair could be settled and
Malcolm covered somehow."

"It takes a lot to rattle Mal Hunter," Felix snapped.

"Nevertheless, he took off in the plane. And once in
Canada, the murderer also killed Malcolm and buried
him there. I saw the grave."

Jan Hunter drew in his breath with a hissing sound.
"Are you certain?"

"I'm guessing. I think it's Malcolm's grave."

There was a curious silence. A low sigh came from
Jan Hunter and he sat down, long angular limbs folded
awkwardly, bald head thrust forward on his bony
shoulders. The firelight reflected on his shiny scalp, his
predatory nose. He smiled and then he stopped smiling
and a puzzled frown touched his shaggy brows. Barney
looked at the other two men. Jason Franklyn kept his
narrow, intellectual face cool and remote. But from Felix
Branthorpe came deep, braying laughter.

"Whatever you're paying this snooper, Jan, it's far too
much. He's out on a limb and he just sawed it off."

Barney felt anger rise in him. "Pitch it out," he said.
If you've got a curve, let's have it."

Felix stood up. His darkly handsome face was venomous with satisfaction. "Mal Hunter isn't dead. Jan hoped
he was, when he hired you. But he isn't. He's very much
alive."

It was as if his words conjured up a looming, shadowy
menace in the firelit room, no less tangible than the three

men who stared at Barney. Jan Hunter looked frightened. Franklyn's face reflected scholarly curiosity. Only Felix seemed to gain satisfaction from what he had said. Despite himself, Barney felt a chill of apprehension.

"You saw Malcolm yourself?" he asked coldly.

Branthorpe nodded. His voice grated. "I saw him, and Evelyn spoke to him on the phone."

"When?"

"This afternoon."

"Did anyone else see him?"

Franklyn wet his thin lips and cleared his throat. "I spoke to Malcolm on the phone, too. Just a few words. He was with Felix then, and Felix came on, afterward. It was enough to convince me."

Barney's face was expressionless, hiding his dismay. "Where is he, then?"

Branthorpe took a step forward. "I told Mal about your little rendezvous with Evelyn last night. He didn't like it. Not at all. He'll settle with you as soon as he can."

"Is he at home?"

"Not yet. But he's right here in Omega."

14

THUNDER rumbled over the mountains. The cool wind had died, and in its place there was a still, dead calm as darkness came. Barney took a cab around the lake to Charley Danger's house, and he was relieved when the flaring headlights cut through the brush to show his rented car still parked in the lane where he had left it. The cab-driver looked curious, but not curious enough to ask questions. Lightning scratched the black sky above the western shore of the lake, then more thunder rolled and rumbled, and a few big drops of warm light rain began to patter on the underbrush as Barney paid off the driver. He stood in the lane until the tail-lights of the taxi disappeared, then turned toward the dark bulk of Danger's house.

Halfway there he paused again as the lightning briefly revealed another car parked down by the float. The rain grew heavier, hissing and rattling in the hazelnut brush that crowded the landing. Barney walked toward the other car and looked it over. It was a small Plymouth coupe, more than ten years old, with one fender awry from an ancient accident. Opening the door, he smelled pipe smoke and stale upholstery. The keys were in the ignition. As he backed out, his thigh brushed against a gun holster permanently fixed to the inside door panel. There was no gun in it.

He looked up at the shimmering windows of Charley Danger's place. No lights shone inside. He didn't think

Evelyn would be waiting there for him again. Turning he walked back to the doorway under the overhang, and he was not surprised when it opened for him before he could use his key.

"Come inside out of the rain, son. I've been waiting for you."

It was Jake Hendrycks. The chief of police bulked heavily in the doorway, his yellow-white hair reflecting the lightning that shimmered over the lake. A crash of thunder shook the earth. Somewhere a branch snapped with a quick rending sound.

Barney went in. Hendrycks snapped on a light and Barney saw the long-barreled revolver in his hand, not pointed precisely at him, but not pointed in any other direction, either.

"What's that for?" he asked.

"I hate to do this, son. Give me your gun."

"Why?"

"You're a dangerous man. You helped Charley Danger to escape and you got him hidden out somewhere. That's what Straehle says. Let's have your gun, Barney."

Barney gave the chief his snubby .38. Hendrycks' pale eyes gave nothing away. He thumbed the cylinder open, shook the barrel down, and looked at the six cartridges inside. He sniffed at the hammer and the barrel.

"You haven't fired this lately, have you?"

"No. Was somebody shot?"

"Why should anybody get shot, Barney?"

"You're acting cagey. How long were you waiting here for me?"

"About ten minutes. I knew you were coming. Kay Franklyn called me the minute you stepped out of the Times office."

Barney nodded. "Who is she, anyway?"

"Third cousin to Jase. Spinster, like he's a bachelor. Used to teach school, then gave it up to devote herself to

Jase. Ain't so closely related they couldn't get married, if Jase was the marrying kind. You know where Charley is, don't you?"

"Not at the moment. You don't believe Charley killed Alex Kane, chief."

Hendrycks scratched at his thick white hair. "Maybe not, but it makes things simple for Straehle. He likes it. He's looked it all over and that's the way he's going to play it, right down the line."

"And you?"

"Mal Hunter is back in town," Hendrycks said heavily.

"Who told you?"

"Jase. I believe it. I can't take a chance otherwise."

"Why is everybody so afraid of Hunter?"

"It ain't fear, exactly. It's different things to different men. Straehle has his ambition. He'll run for governor yet, with Hunter's money behind him. Jase Franklyn's just got no spine; Hunter licked him once and took the paper from him, and he's knuckled under ever since. As for me, I'm getting along in years, son, where the chief's job looks bigger and better to me, with my eight kids to feed and my wife always worrying sick and havin' to scrape and pinch. I don't get paid much, but for an old dodo, it's a good job and I aim to keep it."

"Even at the expense of railroading an innocent man to the chair for murder?"

Hendrycks smiled. His voice was deep and friendly. "You look different, son. You lost some of that hungry look. What happened to you?"

"Many things," Barney said shortly.

"Like Jase says, Omega is the world, and the world is Omega. A man can find what he's looking for, most of the time, right under his nose. Excuse the philosophy, son. I'm just killing time until the rain lets up. I don't like catching colds these days."

"Where is Ferne Kane?" Barney asked.

Hendrycks said gravely: "We don't know. She's gone. Looks like she got a bit scared and lit out for the city. We're looking for her, don't worry about it."

"I'm worried plenty," Barney said. "She knows who killed Alex. She's holed up somewhere until she gets her price. Do you want to come with me to look for her?"

"Not in this rain. And you're going to jail." Hendrycks shook his head. "You sound plumb sure of yourself, about Ferne. You care to tell me about it?"

Barney looked at him with a level stare. "I couldn't trust you now. I don't know how you'd bounce it."

Hendrycks was silent. He lowered his gun, looked at it, shook his head. He looked older, suddenly. "I reckon I've been asking for a remark like that for a long time."

"I'm sorry," Barney said. "You've got something else coming to you."

"And what's that, son?"

"I'm not going to jail tonight."

He struck with no further warning. The chief's gun was lowered, and a quick chopping blow sent it jumping from Hendrycks' hand. It clattered on the floor and as the cop's head came up, his long face agape with surprise, Barney slammed a hard fist to his jaw. Hendrycks grunted, wavered on his feet, and swayed forward, arms flailing. Barney hit him in the middle, chopped at his face, and locked both hands together and slashed down at the back of Hendrycks' neck. The chief hit the floor with the sound of a falling tree.

Barney straightened, breathing deeply.

"I'm really sorry," he whispered.

He picked up the chief's gun and put it on the table, then dipped into Hendrycks' pocket to retrieve his own weapon. A three-celled flashlight was jammed into Hendrycks' back pocket and he took it out, tested it, and kept it. A small trickle of blood came from Hendrycks' lips. He breathed slowly and steadily. Barney felt his pulse, turned him over on his back, and left him there.

Before he quit the house, he took Al Greeley's photograph of Ferne Kane from his pocket. He wished it were daylight, but he had no choice about the time now. He studied the glade and the corner of the white bungalow just visible in one side of the photograph. Through the trees in the picture was a glimmer of water that could be Lake Omega, and a small stream ran through the background. He put the photo away and went outside.

The rain came down in heavy, pounding sheets as he ran for his car. Intermittent lightning flared across the sky, and the air shook with the concussions of thunder over the lake. His rented car gave no trouble in starting. In a matter of minutes he was on his way, driving with care along the twisting road that circled the north end of the lake.

15

ALEX KANE's house and landing looked black under his headlights in the streaming rain. It had taken Barney half an hour of cautious driving, and only now had the thunder and lightning passed over the lake, drifting eastward. The rain still came down heavily. In the glare of his car lights, Kane's house was as dark and deserted as it had been when he came here with Chief Hendrycks the day before. He had not expected anything else.

Using the map-light on the dashboard, he studied the nude photograph of Ferne Kane once more, then folded it decisively and got out of the car. Ignoring the main house, he used Hendrycks' torch to guide his way around to the rear. In a matter of moments he was drenched to the skin by the cold rain. The flashlight caught the glitter of a falling stream of water behind the house and he halted, reconstructing his image of the rocky ledge he had seen when he was here earlier. The tiny waterfall had a drop of about ten feet, and he turned the light to the left and right among the blackly glistening weeds. A small trail began a few feet from where he stood, starting at the edge of the clearing and zigzagging up the ledge. He followed it. At the top, the trail hugged the bank of the stream. Twice he lost the way as he pushed on through the black, thrashing underbrush. For some minutes the rain eased, then came down again in sodden torrents that beat heavily on his shoulders. He could hear nothing above the sounds of the rain and the wind in the woods.

The trail climbed steeply up the mountain slope for a quarter of a mile, and he began to lose hope that his hunch might bear fruit. Then it cut back again, dipped over a shoulder of the hill, and followed the edge of a deep ravine in which the stream flowed far down beneath a tangle of deadfalls. At the head of the ravine his light caught on a broken limb about an inch thick, from an oak sapling that had been uprooted not too long ago. The break in the limb was relatively fresh, although Barney was not woodsman enough to know if it had been done within a matter of hours or days.

A hundred feet farther and higher, he saw the first glimmer of light through the moving branches of the trees above. He halted, and in that moment something flickered in the corner of his eye. Turning, he looked back and down the trail he had followed. There was nothing to see. His flashlight rode back and forth, a feeble effort swallowed by the rain and the night. Everything was distorted, misshapen, in grotesque movement.

He went on. Now and then he lost sight of the lighted window above him, but the trail led generally toward it. When he came to the clearing at the head of a steep outcropping of lichened granite, he halted again. The beam of his flashlight swept back and forth over the wild grass, rested on the bole of a huge, twisted black oak. In the rain, he did not want to take the photograph out. It could be the place, but he was not sure.

The white bungalow just beyond helped decide him.

He had found the spot where Ferne had posed like some debauched woodland nymph for Al Greeley.

Lightning flared, now to the east, now overhead, washing the scene with garish blue glares. At that moment the rain stopped as abruptly as it had begun, as if turned off from a shower tap. Something cracked sharply behind him from the black wall of underbrush at the edge of the clearing.

Instantly Barney thumbed off his light. He was aware of an odd reverbrating *twang!*, then a hiss and chattering of air close to his head. Something thudded into the trunk of the black oak behind him with a vicious sound. As he threw himself flat in the wet wild grass, the twanging snap was repeated and something plucked at his shoulder and went rattling into the brush.

The lightning died and black thunder reverberated over the mountains and the lake far below. Then there was no sound except the drip and patter of rain from wet leaves all around him. He could see nothing. Squirming, he got his gun from his pocket and began to crawl forward, away from the cottage and toward the trail that ended in the glade. The air was filled with the rustling of wet foliage. He paused and waited.

The lightning flickered feebly to the east. Thunder muttered. Then a brilliant flash ribboned across the sky, illuminating the dark, shredded clouds fleeing the upper winds, the steep slope he had just climbed, the twisted wet trunks of trees on either side of the path.

Something white moved and shone and disappeared again.

Barney lunged to his feet, ran twenty steps, then halted as darkness folded in again. The wind pressed his wet clothes flat against his skin. It was useless. Someone was back there in the brush, someone who had followed him or had waited for him here.

Someone with a crossbow, ready to kill him.

He waited. A minute crawled by. Then another. The rain had definitely ended. The thunder was a whimper now, beyond the hills that ringed Lake Omega, and the lightning was only a distant muted flare that leaped and died beyond the oppressive bulk of the mountains.

He waited for ten minutes, and when nothing hap-

pened, he ventured the use of his flashlight, squirting the
beam toward the path for only an instant before clicking
it off. Nothing happened. Nobody stood waiting.

Turning, he walked toward the black oak and again
tried the flashlight. It glistened on the varnished shaft
of an arrow, and on blue pinions. The steel head had
sunk almost out of sight into the iron-hard wood. He
tried to work it out and tug it out, but gave up when the
ash shaft threatened to snap. He could not find the second arrow that had sliced away the clothing on his
shoulder.

There was a queer tingling in his back as he snapped
off the flashlight and let the darkness return over the
glade. He was not convinced that the person who had
tried to kill him had fled the scene. And for the first time
it occurred to him that whereas a hunting long-bow
with perhaps a sixty pound pull would require the
strength of a man, a crossbow did not necessarily de-
mand much strength because of its mechanical features.
No more strength than it took to cock it and pull the
trigger. It could have been a woman back there in the
wet darkness. And he liked this thought even less.

The bungalow was perhaps a hundred feet from where
he stood. The window was still lighted. There had been
no alarm, because he had made no outcry, and the person
who had stalked him had been equally silent. The bungalow was a small affair with a screened porch in front,
dimly lighted by the glow from the window. There was
a yellow quality to the light that indicated it came from
an oil lamp. He did not think there was electric power
wired to this remote fold in the hills. Nobody came to
the door, nobody screamed as he walked toward it.

There was a fieldstone step up to the screened porch.
The door was not locked. The wire spring squealed as
he opened it and stepped to the main entrance. Through
the window he glimpsed a braided rug, rough pine floors,

a fireplace built of rounded, water-smoothed stones, and a seven-point buck's head mounted over the mantel. A fire burned on the hearth behind a smoke-darkened copper screen. He tried the door, found this one locked, and banged on it with his fist.

The rain dripped monotonously all around him. Water gushed and roared in the storm-swollen stream nearby. The thunderstorm was over, and in its place came a breeze of cool air that made him shiver suddenly in his sopping clothes.

He had his hand upraised to knock again when a bolt snapped and the door cracked open about an inch.

Two frightened, careful eyes peered out at him. And another eye, the muzzle of a gun.

"Who is it?" came a whisper.

"Barney Forbes. Let me in, Ferne."

He heard the girl draw a quick, sucking breath. The gun lowered a bit. Not enough to make Barney feel much better, but a little. A chain rattled and the door opened just wide enough for him to slide inside. At once the girl slammed it shut and replaced the chain and the bolt and leaned back against it to stare at him with wide, startled eyes.

"How did you find me?" she breathed.

"Are you here alone?"

"Answer me!" Her voice was taut, like a stretched wire, vibrating with her fear. The gun, however, was ready in her hand. "I want to know how you happened to come here tonight," she demanded. "Not many people know about this place."

"The cops don't, that's for sure."

"You're a cop," she snapped.

"Not exactly. Take it easy, Ferne. I'm here as a friend."

Her tongue came peeking pinkly between her small white teeth. "From Mal?"

"Maybe."

"You lied to me once before."

"The time for lying is past. You're in trouble, and I want to help you. I think I can. But you've got to be sensible, Ferne. You've pushed it alone as far as it will go, and you can't do any more by yourself. You need help."

"Meaning you?" she sneered.

Barney nodded. "Put away the gun. Let's relax."

She lowered the gun, but she did not put it aside. It was comfortable, almost cozy, in the little bungalow. The fire radiated a dry, cheery warmth. The furnishings were simple cheap maple, but the curtains were colorful, the pine paneling was smoked to a friendly patina of age, and the place looked clean. Probably in her isolation for the past twenty-four hours, Ferne had bestirred herself out of boredom to straighten up the place.

Her pale green eyes were wary as Barney crossed the room and threw open the two other doors. One entered into a bedroom, where the bed was rumpled and Ferne's clothes were haphazardly tossed about. The kitchen looked like the kitchen in the lake-front house—disheveled, stacked with empty cans and dirty dishes in the sink. A hand pump dripped water on the heap of stacked china. The back door was locked. Barney turned back and looked at the blonde girl.

In the glow of the two oil lamps and the firelight, she looked surprisingly fresh and innocent, except for her suspicious, too-knowing eyes. Perhaps it was because she hadn't bothered with makeup, being alone, and her mouth had a clean, pink look. A simple blue ribbon tied up her blonde hair in a pony's-tail. She wore old sneakers, skin-tight denim slacks rolled up to her knees, and an equally tight, red pullover sweater. Obviously, she wore nothing else under it. Barney looked away from her to the windows. There were no shades, and only narrow striped drapes hung on either side, too narrow to be closed to blot out the night beyond. He frowned, worried.

"Get in a corner where you can't be seen, Ferne."

"Why?" she asked, her tone belligerent.

"Somebody is out there. With Alex's crossbow, I think. He—or she—sent a couple of arrows after me." He looked at her closely. Her sneakers were dry. "Was it you?"

"I haven't stuck my nose out of this dump since yesterday. And I don't believe you."

"Do you mind if *I* stand away from the windows, then?"

She looked scornful. "Are you afraid?"

"I just don't like being a sitting target," he said. "You can suit yourself." He ignored her gun, choosing a maple rocker in a corner of the pine-paneled room.

The girl looked undecided. Again the tip of her tongue wet her lips. Her eyes glistened, reflecting the firelight. "You're not just trying to scare me?"

"You've got enough to be afraid of, doing what you're trying to do, for me to have to add anything to it," Barney said quietly. "You're in a bad spot, and you know it, or you wouldn't be hiding out here."

"You still haven't told me how you found me."

"We'll come to it. Have you seen Mal yet?"

She tossed her head in defiance. "No. But I will."

"I don't think so. Who else have you tried to contact?"

"What are you talking about?"

"Blackmail," he said, and her face tightened. "You know who killed Alex, and you know what happened to Malcolm Hunter that night, too. You've got something to sell, but you don't want to sell cheap. You think this is your big chance to clean up. But it's a dangerous game and you're alone in it, and you're apt to wind up with Alex—with rocks tied to your beautiful body and ten feet of water over your head."

"You can't scare me," she whispered. "I know what I'm doing."

"I hope so. How did you know that Mal Hunter flew up to Lake Quenniboscet that night?"

"That's my business. He—" She paused, biting her lip, her green eyes hot with quick anger. "That's a cop's trick." She crossed the room to stand at the fireplace, her body sleek and undulant in her tight clothes. Her yellow pony-tail swung sharply as she turned to face him again. She smiled. "You think you're so smart. Well, I'm smarter than you think—smarter than the rest of them. Sure, I know what happened that night And I'm going to make it pay off for yours truly, in a big way! I know what people say about me—and I'm going to ram it all back down their teeth."

"A lot of it is true, isn't it?" Barney asked quietly.

She glared at him. "What of it? If men like what I've got and are willing to give me what I want, I'm willing to make a deal any time." Her pink mouth curled in contempt. "You think you're so high and mighty, how come *you* don't know what happened that night?"

"I expect to find out," he said.

"How?" she snapped.

"From Al Greeley," he told her quietly.

Her lips parted. She started to speak, then swallowed and turned away. He could not see her face when she spoke. Her voice was a dull whisper. "What about Al?"

"You know him, don't you?"

"Yes."

"You know him well?"

"I guess you have the answer to that one."

Barney nodded. "And I have the photograph he took of you. That's how I found you."

She was silent. For a moment her shoulders sagged. Barney waited, listening to the drip of rain off the roof

eaves, the patter of quick drops as the wind shook
the brush outside. When the girl turned back to him,
her mouth was sullen, her eyes defiant.

"Al isn't the only man I knew or had fun with. You
talk as if there's something special about him with me,
but there isn't. I could tell you plenty about some of the
old goats in this town who chase after me, offering me
all kinds of things." Her voice grew strong with scorn.
"I could name a lot of names that would bust this town
wide open. Al isn't important. Not to me. That was over
and done with a long time ago."

"How long ago?"

"I don't know." She pretended to consider. "I guess
I saw him last about a year ago."

"You're lying," he said. He took the photograph from
his pocket. "This snapshot was taken recently."

"Give that to me," she whispered.

"It would be easy for a lab expert to check the underbrush growth shown in this film and figure when the
shot was taken," Barney said. He saw her eyes widen.
"You know what I'm getting at, Ferne. I told you I
want to help you, and the only way I can do that is if
you level with me. You expect to get a lot of money from
the murderer who killed Alex. You know his name.
Have you contacted him yet?"

She tossed her head. "He'll pay me plenty!"

"Or he might kill you," Barney said softly.

Her mouth curled. "Him? I'm not afraid of him. The
way he comes crawling and whining! If you knew who
he was—" She checked herself. "I don't want to talk to
you any more. You have no right to be here. I've done
nothing wrong. I came up here to be alone, that's all.
That's my story if the cops come."

Barney said: "You found out who killed Alex from
Greeley, didn't you?"

"I won't talk to you any more."

He stood up. "Didn't you?" he demanded.

"Stay away from me!"

"Answer me, Ferne. Al did a job for the murderer and you wheedled the truth out of him. You got it the day you let him take that photo of you. Isn't that the truth?"

"No!"

"You're still lying. If I must, I'll turn this picture over to the cops and the newspapers. They won't print it, but they'll talk about it plenty. What good would your money do then, if you got any? Where could you go where your reputation wouldn't follow you?"

Her eyes were wide. "You wouldn't. . . ."

"Try me," he warned.

"People will forget. . . ."

"But not the murderer," Barney said.

For a moment more she tried to be brazen and angry. Then abruptly her face crumpled and a deep, shuddering sob wracked her body. She cried without sound, her chest heaving, tears flowing down her cheeks. The transformation from a brash, amoral siren to a small, frightened girl was startling. She dropped the gun to her side. Barney moved at once, caught her wrist, twisted, and took the gun from her. It was a small pearl-handled .28, a purse-fitting husband-killer. He drew a deep breath as he pocketed it.

"Now tell me the truth," he said quietly.

"Damn you," she whispered. "I wasn't afraid at all, until you came here. I was doing all right. . . ."

"You were only kidding yourself. Stop crying. And start talking."

She turned blindly toward him, leaning against him, her face against his chest. He felt pity for her small, sordid dreams, her petty ambitions that were built out of the limited world she knew, her greed and what would be her inevitable disappointment.

Then, without warning, she brought her knee up in a

savage thrust that exploded blinding pain inside him.

He cried out in shock and pain, reeled backward. His legs tangled with a chair and he went down, conscious only of his agony. Above the roaring in his ears he heard Ferne's high, shrill laughter. Her face wavered above him, twisted with triumph and hate. When she leaped toward him, kicking and biting and scratching, he rolled away, struggling to draw in a relieving breath. Her words were incoherent as she clawed at him, but through the vituperation the gist of it was plain enough. She hated men. All men. For her, Barney was the symbol of the brutal, grasping sex that had ruled her life. Her voice was a screaming tirade that gradually came clearer through the haze of pain in him. He filled his lungs at last and pushed her weight from him.

Then there was silence.

Her screams of rage ended as abruptly as if cut off with a knife. Barney started to rise, a sudden panic in him. He saw Ferne back away, hands outthrust, palms out, as if to push something from her. Her face was white, unrecognizable. She was looking at something beyond him, in the kitchen doorway.

He had no chance to turn around. There was an instant when he heard a quick step, a rustle of wet clothing, and then something struck the back of his head and he pitched forward, falling over and over into a dark, whirling emptiness.

16

Voices reached for him, voices that sobbed and pleaded, voices that argued angrily.

He could not move. He seemed to live somewhere in a place of darkness, as if his conscious ego were detached from reality. Pain washed through him and fought his desire to let everything go and sink back into the oblivion from which he had drifted. There was dust in his throat, a smell of wet wool, crackling sounds, and the voices. The pain convinced him he was still alive, awake but not entirely awake.

There was a voice that was scornful, rejecting, acid with contempt. A woman, talking rapidly, refusing something. He thought it was Ferne, but he could not be sure. He tried to raise his head, but he could move no part of him, and then panic overwhelmed his interest in the two voices and he lost touch with them. When they registered again, the scornful voice was laced with growing terror. Its tone had changed to sobs and pleas.

He listened to the other voice. He could not identify it. It was as if the owner spoke through an echo chamber, and the words came to him in garbled fashion, strangely distorted. He knew it was important for him to understand what was being said, to recognize the speakers. The darkness dragged him down and away from them, before he could summon more strength to listen acutely.

The voices ebbed and were gone.

For a time, there was nothing.

119

When he again became aware of the dust and the smell of wool, he knew at once that this was true reality. He did not make any effort to move. He was sprawled face down on the braided rug of Ferne's bungalow, and he kept his eyes closed, trying to breathe as he had been breathing, trying to sense if anyone was near.

He had a feeling of emptiness and desertion.

He opened his eyes.

His gaze focused slowly on his right hand, near his face, and he studied it as if it belonged to a stranger. His fingers were clenched around smooth wood, a longish rectangle inlaid with intricate designs of nacre and enamel. Beyond it was an ornate curve of black, polished wood attached to the stock he gripped.

He sat up with a lurch, his heart pounding.

Someone had fixed a crossbow in his hand.

Pain shook him, and he groaned aloud as his vision blurred. Something soft and warm and smooth yielded under his left hand as he pushed up from the floor. Deep and ugly horror crawled over him. He drew back quickly, sweat pouring from him, as he looked at the body.

It was Ferne Kane.

Her face was battered and bruised, fixed in an expression of ultimate horror. Her eyes were chips of bright glass, glittering in the dim light of the dying fire. It was cold in the room now. The tight sweater she had worn was ripped from her, and her tanned semi-naked body was streaked and lacerated as if some savage animal had mauled her in berserk rage. Through her left breast protruded the shaft of the now-familiar arrow. Only a small trickle of blood came from the wound.

Nausea gripped him, churned inside him. He tasted bitter acid in the back of his mouth. Abruptly he released his hold on the odd, Oriental weapon in his grip.

Then he felt caution, and a sense of pressing danger.

He tried to stand, groaned with the pain in his head, and rested again, gasping. There was only silence in the room, shared with the murdered girl. He had the feeling that much time had passed, but when he looked at his watch he saw it was only eleven o'clock, less than an hour since he had arrived. He pushed himself up again, and this time stood waveringly on his feet.

His gun was gone, along with Ferne's and the photo of Ferne. One of the oil lamps had burned out, exhausting its fuel, and odd shadows filled the room, emphasized by the glow of dying coals on the fireplace. He shivered violently.

When he moved into the kitchen, he saw that the back door stood open to the yawning night. The trees still dripped rain from the recent thunderstorm. He looked at the lock, but it had not been broken. Whoever had come while Ferne struggled with him had had a key. The key could only have come from Ferne. Given to a friend. But she had many male friends. It could have been anyone. Barney's thoughts moved sluggishly around the problem, and then he turned to the sink, pushed the heaped dishes aside, and used the hand pump to pour gushing cold water over his head. It helped. He groped for a towel and dried his scalp gingerly, feeling for the wound on the back of his head. His scalp was lacerated and had bled a little, but it did not seem serious. The pain in him was ebbing rapidly.

As his senses sharpened, his feeling of imminent danger increased. Another wave of nausea shook him and as he paused, his glance captured a small, golden gleam on the braided rug in the living room, near the fireplace. He went to it and picked up the object.

It was a small sunburst watchfob on a finely linked chain of gold. He frowned, trying to remember where he had seen a similar piece of jewelry before. His first visit to the Hunter estate came back to him, and he recalled a necklace Evelyn Hunter had worn, with a similar sunburst on a fine golden neck chain. Barney's mouth went dry. There was a catch on the fob, and he thumbed it open. Inside, in ornate scrolled letters, were the initials *M. H.* Malcolm Hunter. A tiny photo of Evelyn stared at him.

Again Barney felt as if a looming image had been conjured up out of the shadows, huge and menacing. The fine links of the watchfob chain had been rudely torn, as if they had caught on something in the struggle and had been ripped away.

Pocketing the ornament, he started toward the body of the dead girl—and then abruptly paused.

Danger, danger, danger!

He stood frozen, listening.

Brush crackled outside. A man called softly. Another man answered in a deep, annoyed growl.

Instantly Barney flashed around, crossing the kitchen with a long stride to slip outside through the open back door. Dark shadows enveloped him as he flattened against the bungalow wall. He began to shake and he recognized the grip of panic and tried to fight it off. He was not completely successful.

"Forbes!"

Barney edged to the corner and looked out over the dark glade. Flashlights winked, and a large bull's-eye electric lantern sent a sudden, stabbing beam over the bungalow. The shadows of four or five men moved across the wet clearing, rifles held in the crooks of their arms.

"He must be in there! He killed the girl!"

It was Straehle's voice.

The whole picture formed in detail in Barney's mind then. The murderer had anticipated that Straehle, informed of Ferne's hideout, would surprise Barney there with Ferne's body. Whether any serious attempt could

be made to pin the murder on Barney was not the point.
But it would certainly take him out of the case, which
was the murderer's aim. Evidently the previous attempt
on his life, with the crossbow, had been revised. In
jail, charged with implication in Ferne's death, the
waters would be muddied to the murderer's satisfaction
and serve a better purpose than Barney's death. But he
received a small grain of satisfaction from his swift
thoughts. It meant the murderer was now afraid, and the
corollary to that was that Barney knew something dangerous to the killer or was moving into an area where the
murderer could take no further chances with what he
might learn.

"Forbes!"

Straehle's yell was sharp and brittle against the night
silence. Barney pressed flat against the bungalow for a
moment as heavy footsteps mounted the front porch. A
flashlight flickered on the black, wet grass nearby. He
heard another command, another shout—and then he
ran.

He was halfway across the clearing before he was
spotted. A man yelled, another took it up. He forced his
legs to a burst of speed. The distance to the sheltering
brush seemed infinite. A rifle cracked, but the bullet went
wide. He threw himself forward, panting, in the darkness. In a moment, all of Straehle's men were in pursuit.

There was moonlight, shining intermittently through
the dark, shredded clouds fleeing overhead. At first he
had no destination in mind. His only goal was to escape
the armed men behind him. When he fell, tripping over
a root, he picked himself up and ran on again. His legs
were weak, and he felt blood start from his scalp
wound again. He did not stop. His lungs seemed to be
on fire. Then, without warning, the ground vanished
under his stumbling footsteps and he fell through empty

space, forcing back a yell of surprise that sprang from his throat. Branches tore and lashed at him as he rolled down a steep, rocky slope. He let himself go, tumbling loosely through the tangled underbrush. He was brought up short against a clump of white birches with a force that slammed the breath out of him.

He could not get up again. For long moments the earth and sky reeled overhead, while he sprawled and struggled to pump air into his lungs. Over the pulsing in his ears he heard several spiteful rifle shots, and then more shouts from Straehle's men. But the voices were far away and above him, and he did not stir. Presently, too, he heard the quick gushing chuckle of the mountain stream as it plunged toward the lake far below.

He sat up. His arms trembled, his body felt as if it had been used for a punching bag. Lights glimmered above as he looked up, then they vanished. The shouts grew dim, moving up the dark mountainside. After another moment he stood up, resting against the slim birches, and then climbed slowly down the rough slope, following the sound of the stream.

The flashlight he had taken from Hendrycks had been lost, and he had to wait now and then for the fitful gleam of the moon when it appeared between the torn clouds. Now and then a cold wind shook the trees and sent down showers of rainwater. He picked his way down with dogged persistence. Time was lost, stretching without end one moment, then compressed into nothing at all. He had no idea how long it was before he glimpsed the lake and then a light from Kane's landing. He paused warily at the head of the waterfall. The light came from Alex Kane's house, but he saw no movement inside. Evidently Straehle and his men had searched here first. His glance covered the lane where he had parked his car. It was still there. Two others were behind it. But he spotted no movement, no challenging guard left behind.

He descended to the lane with caution. Shadows moved
and jumped in the wind, scattering rain drops, rattling
branches. He saw no one, heard nothing. Then, as he
was only a few feet from his rented coupe, he spotted
the man sprawled face down in the mud.

It was one of the deputies. His rifle lay a few feet
from where he had fallen, and he did not move as
Barney approached.

Barney knelt beside him for only a moment, long
enough to see the matted blood on the back of the deputy's head. The guard had been slugged.

He straightened in quick alarm again. Somebody
laughed softly and he whirled to face the sound.

It was the two hoodlums, the fat little man and the
vicious boy he had met when he first arrived in Omega.

17

"So you got away from the cops," the fat man said. He smiled cheerfully. "We didn't think you'd make it."

Barney stood still. They both had guns and this time they kept a wary distance from him. In the moonlight, he saw the face of the nervous one twitch irregularly. They wore raincoats, and the moon made anonymous wedges of their faces, although he could make out the saddle nose on the older, more experienced fat man, and the spasms of anger on the younger man's features.

"Take it easy, Henry," he said to the latter.

"You son of a bitch," Henry rasped. "This time we fix you."

The fat man said: "Henry, he's right. Remember last time, when you lost your head."

"I want to kill him," said Henry.

The fat man chuckled. "You may get your chance. But not now. Not yet."

"Just who are you working for?" Barney asked.

"There is no harm in your knowing. Malcolm Hunter gives the orders in Omega."

"Through Branthorpe?"

"I think we had better go now, before Straehle realizes you've doubled back for your car," said the fat man. "You look as if you've had a hard time."

Barney did not move. "Tell me more about Hunter. When did you see him last?"

Henry said: "If I kill him now, Chaz, I'd be doing the cops a favor."

"Heaven forbid," said the fat man. "There's time enough for your fun later. Let's go."

The deputy lying in the mud nearby began to groan and move his limbs spasmodically. Henry turned to him with an annoyed sound. At the same moment, the moon began to slide behind the clouds again.

"Where are we going?" Barney asked.

"Maybe to Hunter," said Chaz, grinning. "He's got some business with you."

The moon vanished. Darkness came as if a curtain had been drawn over the scene. Henry was bending over the fallen deputy when Barney drew a deep breath and suddenly dived behind his car. The fat man yelled and as Henry straightened, Barney stiff-armed him and sent him reeling into his companion. The fat man's gun went off, slamming into the trees.

Barney ran.

For a few seconds he knew he was a fairly clear target for the hoodlums. But no other shots followed. Evidently Chaz and Henry had no more desire than he to draw the cops to the scene. The brush plucked and clawed at him again. He plunged on, following the lane to the road. He did not look back. For a minute or two he heard footsteps and shouts behind him, then they ended and he halted for breath at the edge of the main road.

The moon came out, flooding the night with silver. Nobody followed him. He was trembling with fatigue as he started walking toward town.

He walked for almost an hour, halting to hide once when Straehle's police cars roared by. It was after midnight. He had passed several cottages, all dark with slumber, and all the cars he spotted and investigated were tightly locked. Anger walked with him as he trudged down the dark road. Then his first break came when he noted the rural mailbox before a prim little bungalow near the edge of town. In lettering was the name: *K. Franklyn*. He paused. The bungalow was dark, but the doors to the garage were wide open and no car was visible. Katydids shrilled their undulating chorus in the treetops. Then from the road toward town came the sound of an approaching car that slowed as its headlights swept the curve and touched the white bungalow.

Barney waited in the sheltering shadow of a nearby tree. He was not sure what he could gain by talking to Franklyn's receptionist, but it was better than another hour of walking. The car turned into the driveway and halted, then eased into the garage. A light flicked on over the front entrance to the bungalow and Kay Franklyn came out of the garage and walked to her house. She wore a transparent plastic raincoat, with the hood tossed back over her gray hair. Keys jingled in her hand as Barney stepped from the shadows and spoke to her.

"Don't be alarmed, Miss Franklyn."

She gave a quick gasp and whirled to face him, eyes wide with fright. "What are you doing here?"

"Walking back to town," he said. He tried to smile, but his face hurt. "Did you think the police had me?"

"I heard that Straehle was after you," she said. She wore a severe gray business suit under the raincoat. She drew a quick, uncertain breath. "I have nothing to say to you. From your looks, you're on the run. Don't ask me to help. I have no sympathy whatever."

Barney blocked her way with his arm across the door. "I'm afraid I must insist on your help. Why do you resent me?"

"I don't. You mean nothing to me."

"Except as a threat to Jason, isn't that true?"

Her mouth tightened. Her eyes retreated from his gaze. "You are a threat to no one in Omega, Mr. Forbes. Certainly not to Jason. He has nothing to fear. He is honest and fine and good—"

"A total Boy Scout in your eyes," Barney said. "Are you in love with him?"

"You are impertinent," she snapped.

"And curious," he said. "What were you doing in town so late?"

"Is that any of your business?"

"I'm making it mine."

"You will learn nothing from me. Please go away. I am not afraid of you. If you stay another moment I'll start screaming."

"Go ahead," he said flatly. "Scream."

She stood facing him, anger in her face, and something beyond the anger that slowly surfaced and made her shoulders less firm, her attitude less adamant. She looked at the road. When she spoke, it was in a small, tired voice.

"What is it you want? I know nothing. I can't help you."

"You can tell me where Jason was tonight," he said.

"At home!" she said sharply.

"How do you know?"

"I—I worked late at the office. I often do. I would have known it if he went out. I always know."

"Are you sure?"

Her eyes glistened. "I watch over him all the time. I try to see that he has whatever he needs. He doesn't know about it. Sometimes I think he doesn't even know I exist."

"What about Jan Hunter?" Barney asked gently.

She seemed relieved. "Mr. Hunter is returning to New York on the late train—the 12:50."

"Tonight?"

"Yes. His decision was quite sudden."

Barney looked at his watch. It was twenty minutes

before train time. A sense of urgency possessed him. "Why is he leaving?"

"He is afraid, Mr. Forbes." The woman seemed to grow taller, her voice reflecting quiet triumph. "He is afraid of Mal Hunter. Just as you should be."

"Look, I want to see Jan before he goes. Would you drive me to the station?"

"I'm afraid I—"

"It's important, Miss Franklyn."

She looked at him curiously. "Are you quite all right? You look rather battered. If the police are after you, I don't really think I should—"

"Give me your keys, then."

She hesitated. "Very well. But you should see a doctor, Mr. Forbes. You—"

He took her keys from her hand. "Thanks." He started for the car, then turned to her as she stood in the doorway. "I hope I don't run into the police at the station, Miss Franklyn. If I do, I'll know you called them."

Her mouth was a tight, prim line. "I have not decided whether to call them or not. You will have to take that chance."

"I could take you with me."

"You had better hurry, Mr. Forbes."

He hesitated, then saw no help for it. He ran to the car. As he backed out of the driveway, clashing gears in the old coupe, he saw her still standing before her house. An odd little smile touched her mouth, and then she was gone.

Omega was asleep, wrapped in midnight darkness except for a row of lighted windows in the courthouse from Straehle's office. Barney drove by the courthouse square, turned and went two blocks to the railroad depot. There was no activity at the station, but the lights still shining over the roofed waiting platform indicated that the last train had not yet arrived. No cars were in the parking area. The depot building itself was locked and dark.

For a moment he thought the station was completely deserted. Then a sudden movement far down the platform, near a baggage trailer, showed him Jan Hunter. Barney turned, walked swiftly down the wooden platform. From far beyond the looming mountains came the distant wail of a train whistle.

"Hunter!" he called.

Jan Hunter turned as if to run, then came toward him, carrying a small traveling grip. His face looked gaunt and yellow under the tin-shaded platform lights.

"Good Lord. I thought the police had you!"

"Not yet," Barney said grimly. "Why are you running out?"

"I think it is the wisest course. What happened to your face?"

"Never mind that. Were you with Franklyn all evening?"

"Not entirely. I went to Mal's house to talk to Evelyn."

"Not with Ferne?"

"Certainly not. Really, Forbes, I think now that I've made a serious mistake. Malcolm certainly needs no help from me. Perhaps Branthorpe is right. He will be angry at my interference. I'm sorry about this, but I no longer need your services."

"You mean I'm fired?" Barney asked grimly.

"I'll pay your full fee, of course, but I would appreciate it if you forgot the entire matter and returned to New York at once."

"You can't forget murder. And the police aren't going to forget about me, here in Omega or wherever I go. Whether I work for you or not, I'm staying. And you would be wise to stay, too."

The eagle's face looked shattered. "Why did you ask me about Ferne?"

"Somebody killed her tonight. Didn't you know?"

Jan Hunter made a small sound in his throat. "No," he whispered. "I didn't— I wasn't aware—"

"The local cops will think it pretty strange if you take off into the wild blue tonight. Just why are you running?"

"I'm afraid of my brother, Mr. Forbes. It's as simple as that," Jan whispered.

The train whistle sounded again, louder, and there was a singing vibration in the steel rails that curved past the platform. Jan stared beyond him with such force that Barney instinctively turned his head. Nothing was visible along the bleak, deserted platform.

"I must go back," Jan whispered. "I can't face him."

"Mal is dead," Barney said bluntly.

"But you're wrong! I spoke to him myself, on the phone! It was Mal."

"What did he want?"

"Nothing much. He asked me how I was. And he laughed. But when I requested an explanation—he hung up."

"Where and when did you get this call?"

"Tonight. About ten o'clock. After you and Felix left. It was at Jason's. I thought Mal had called from his house, so I went there. But Evelyn had not seen him. She's afraid, too. So I came back to Jason's to pack."

"Was Franklyn at home then?"

"I don't know. I didn't see him. But it's a large house and I was deliberately quiet. The only person who saw me was Kay." Jan's mouth shook with sudden fear. Barney felt confused. He had been so sure he was right. But in the face of this, he felt as if everything he had counted on was falling apart. Some of the other man's fear touched him, too. He did not understand it. It was as if Mal Hunter, dead or alive, had the power of an evil shadow over all of Omega. A wave of despair swept him, compounded of frustration and fatigue. He knew too much about police work, even in a small town like Omega, to hope to stay free much longer. Defeat loomed on every side.

A distant rumbling shook the platform as the train rounded the long curve into the station. Jan Hunter was the only passenger waiting to board the New York express. The massive beam of the locomotive headlight swept over them like a scythe, lighting Jan's long, pallid face. Terror had etched deep lines on it, collapsing the front of the city clubman, the *bon vivant*, the confident man of wealth. As the locomotive thundered by, hissing and monstrous, Hunter suddenly caught Barney's arm.

"I'll stay. But you must help me!" he shouted over the din. "If they ever find out about Ferne—"

Steam hissed with a shattering noise for a moment.

"What about Ferne?" Barney demanded.

"She came to New York once. To talk to me about Mal, she said. She—she appealed to me. She seemed such a charming child. I—I took her to a few places, dinner and clubs. She stayed—she wouldn't go home for three days."

"When was this?"

"Two months ago. I swear I never saw her again, after that! But if the police—"

The train had halted and the conductor, swinging from the open door of a nearby coach, looked at them expectantly. A jet of steam plumed up from under the steps, obscuring him. But Jan Hunter was not looking that way. His hand fell from Barney's arm. His mouth opened, then closed. Another spasm of terror distorted his face. A bell clanged, the conductor closed the coach door, and the train rumbled forward. Jan Hunter gave a little cry and suddenly twisted away from Barney and began running away down the platform.

Barney looked at the parking area. Two men were coming his way. They were unmistakable. Fat little Chaz and nervous Henry. There was purpose in their bearing, and recklessness in the way they held their guns openly. The light flickered from the windows of the passing train and the air shook again as the last coach pulled away from the platform.

Barney stepped back onto the shimmering steel tracks.

"Don't try it!" Chaz called over the diminishing roar.

Beyond the tracks was a high board fence, curving with the curve of the roadbed for a hundred feet in either direction. Barney looked quickly for Jan Hunter. He was gone. His bag still stood on the station platform.

There was no place to go.

He stood still as the two gunmen approached.

18

HE AWOKE to daylight, and for a moment there was bleak confusion in his mind. The light shone blindingly in his eyes from a small square window set in a rough, unfinished wall. A spade, a garden rake, a length of hose hung from hooks in the studding beside the window. The air felt intolerably hot and close. He started to raise his arm to look at his watch and found himself helpless, bound hand and foot to the cot on which he lay.

It came back to him then, the swift drive up the mountainside with Chaz and Henry, the shack where they stopped, and Henry's blunt attentions. It explained, together with his memory of flight from Ferne's place, the dull ache of bruises all through his body.

He turned his head and examined the rest of the room. There was a weathered pine table, two chairs, some empty liquor bottles, and a kerosene space heater. Through the window he saw the dark blue-green of a huge spruce against the brazen sky. It was about noon, he judged, and he was aware of hunger and thirst.

He had not dreamed of Lil, for the first time in a year.

He listened to the silence, and then he slept again.

An hour later, Chaz woke him by lightly slapping his face. "Hey, Forbes. Hey, now. Let's have a little talk."

The fat man wore a gaudy yellow sport shirt with the tails hanging over creamy slacks. His face was badly sunburned, and his saddle nose was peeling. He looked hot and troubled as he pulled a chair scrapingly across the floor and sat down. Dust lifted from the rough planks and eddied in the shaft of sunlight that fell on the cot.

"How do you feel, Forbes?"

"Numb."

"Ropes too tight?"

"Take them off."

"Sorry. Orders. You got away twice. Three times and I'm out. You're lucky Henry didn't kill you last night. I can't always control that boy. He'll be along later, and I'd advise you not to rile him. Having Henry is like holding a tiger by the tail."

"Why keep me here?" Barney asked. "I don't have anything you want."

"Information," Chaz said. He sighed, took a violet handkerchief from his creamy slacks and mopped his face, wincing from the raw areas of peeling skin on his nose. "We want to know about your trip to Canada."

"Who is we?"

"The boss. You know. You behave, and after a day or so we let you go. Button up, and you're lucky if we don't arrange for you to go to the slammer. You hungry?"

"I could eat. I could drink. I could take a walk."

Chaz laughed. "I like you. For a cop, I like you. I must be getting stupid in my old age. Henry would be stacked off, hearing you talk like that. You want to tell me about your trip to Canada?"

"I'll tell the boss," Barney said. "Send him in."

"Are you stupid?" Chaz asked.

"Just stubborn. Ask him."

"You see him and you get dead," Chaz said earnestly. "You think he lets you go, once you peep him? Talk to me. Who's dead up in Canada?"

"What do you know about it?" Barney asked.

"I got questions to ask. About Canada, who was up

there, about who got killed and buried up there."

"Can I have a drink of water?" Barney asked.

"Sure thing," Chaz said cheerfully. He went out of the room. Barney caught only a brief glimpse of the next room, which seemed to be as barren as this one. Through the closed window he heard the muted singing of birds, the distant drone of a plane. There was nothing else to see except the spruce tree and the hot blue sky. Chaz came back with a glass of water and stood beside the cot. "Real thirsty?"

"Yes."

"Have it, then."

He poured the water slowly over the floor, laughing to himself. "Understand this, Forbes. No food, no water, nothing but aches and pains, until you tell us what you found up there in Canada."

"To hell with you," Barney said.

The rest was pain, quick and violent. He lived in a red nightmare while Chaz deftly did things to his helpless body, operating with a clinical efficiency like that of a surgeon. After less than a minute, Barney welcomed the deep tidal wave of darkness that came over him.

Voices.
Who tipped you to Canada?
Where is Hunter?
Was he up there?
TELL US!
Don't be stupid.
Where is Hunter?
Pain . . .
Lil was with him. She came out of the dark, eyes glowing, lips parted and smiling. Just for him. There was no sadness, no tears. It was good. She talked to him with the quiet, womanly serenity of mind and body she always had, and he tried to hear what she said, but the dis-

*tance and the darkness between them was too deep. But
it was all right. It was fine. Under her talk there was sadness and some resignation, and a sense of waiting. And
while he looked at her, feeling a dreadful burden lift
from his soul, she became Evelyn, and he was back at
Charley Danger's house with her, and that was good,
too. The two were one, and sometimes more than one,
and finally Lil went away, dark veils falling between
them slowly, then faster and faster, until he could not
see her any more and he knew he would not see her
again, and that was the way she wanted it to be.*

The room was dark again. He came back to hunger and
thirst and scalding pain. Chaz was clever with his hands.
Much worse than Henry's wild, animal ferocity. Chaz
was an artist, and Barney knew that if he lived through
this he would find Chaz again somewhere, and kill him.
Chaz began to know this, too, and worry made him
less capable, made him angry so that subtlety no longer
had a chance of working. Barney did not know why he
refused to tell him about the grave in Canada. Chaz told
him, time and again, that he had nothing to lose. Once
he heard another man's voice in the next room, muttering in anger. Then Chaz came back and demanded
with shrill violence to know if Malcolm Hunter was still
alive.

For perhaps two hours afterward he was left alone.
His arms and legs were numb, and he saw the limit of his
endurance fast approaching. He knew that when he
spoke, more than this would be ended. He told himself
not to speak, to wait.

There was a sharp, querulous voice outside the cabin
then, a gasp, a thud. The outer door opened. Another
curse, a grunt, another thudding sound, as if a man had
fallen to the floor. Light flickered under the door, went
away, came back again. Soft footsteps prowled lightly

about.

Barney waited. His pulse quickened and he strained to identify the sounds. When the door opened on rusted hinges, he could see nothing beyond the glare of a flashlight shining in his eyes.

"Barney?"

He summoned strength from inside him. "Who is it?"

"Charles Danger."

"Look out for—"

"They're out—both of them. Don't worry. Jesus, you took a beating!"

"How did you find me?"

"I hung around Hunter's place and followed the thin one here. I've been in the woods since Jackson. Got a little surprise for you." Danger deftly cut at Barney's bonds with a hunting knife. The flashlight, resting on the floor, made his narrow face all angular, his eyes savage. The knife flickered in the light, and then he sheathed it. "Can you stand up?"

"I don't know."

"Come on. I'll help you."

"Where is Chaz?" Barney asked.

"When he comes to, he'll have a headache."

"When he comes to, I'll kill him," Barney said.

Danger whistled as he examined Barney more closely. "I wouldn't blame you. Try to walk now, eh?"

His legs were rubbery under him, full of prickling, tingling pain. He tried to stand. Danger held him up. He tried again, and sweat broke out all over him. His eyes smarted. His mouth was puffed and there was dried blood on his hands.

"Just a couple of steps more. We'll have to hurry."

"What time is it?"

"Early. Nine o'clock. How long have you been here?"

"Since last night."

"And they both worked you over?"

"Their boss is anxious to know for sure if Hunter is alive or dead. I didn't tell them."

"Everybody in town thinks Hunter is back," Danger said. "But nobody has seen him except Branthorpe."

"Do you believe it?"

"We'll talk about it later. Hang on."

The night air was cool, scented by the pines. Barney dragged in deep, reviving breaths. The sweat began to dry on his face. "How far do we have to go?"

"Three miles, mostly downhill, back toward the lake. Can you make it?"

"I'll make it," Barney said. He looked at the sprawled figure of Henry, on the grass outside the shack, and at Chaz, just within the threshold. They had both been knocked out with the silence and speed of a jungle animal. He drew another deep breath and felt strength returning to him. He said again: "I'll make it. Then I'll come back."

They followed a hiking trail down the face of the mountain. In the moonlight, the lake could be seen far below, with the town of Omega on the far side like a distant and unreal stage setting. As Barney walked, he felt stronger with each step, although he knew he was no match at the moment for a ten-year-old. But at least he was able to walk without Danger's help after the shack was out of sight.

"How is Straehle doing?" Barney asked.

"He's looking for you. He says now it's for your own good, before Hunter gets you." Danger's voice grew cool. "Why would Mal be set on killing you, Barney?"

"Because of Evelyn," he said quietly.

"Why Evelyn?"

"She spent most of that night with me," Barney said. "At your place."

Danger halted. "I don't believe you."

"She had a key. We talked. I kissed her. It wasn't much more than that. She fell asleep there and left before you showed up. But Felix prowled around and spotted her. That's where it started."

The Indian drew a deep, whistling breath. "I'm in love with her. You know that, don't you?"

"I've guessed it. And she's in love with you. It doesn't have to bother me, Charley. And it doesn't bother me that the story is going around that I played around with her and that's why Hunter is after me. I don't think it troubles Evelyn, either."

"That's why I stopped working for Hunter. I couldn't take it any more," Danger said. "Neither could Evelyn. Being so close to each other, and having that filthy brute torment her and ignore her and hurt her, in a thousand ways, day in and day out. I wanted to kill him. I was afraid I would. That's why I left."

"Don't hand that one to Straehle," Barney told him. "You'll hang for sure. That's why I'd rather let Straehle think Evelyn was in your place because of me. Branthorpe must have told him."

"You still think Hunter is dead? In that grave we found?"

"I'm sure of it," Barney said. "Tonight I'll prove it."

"Did you know Ferne was killed?" the Indian asked abruptly.

"Yes. She was cozy with Al Greeley. When we find him, we'll get the answers we need."

"I've found him," Danger said quietly. "Come on."

19

BARNEY's rented car was parked beside the rustic cabin where Danger halted. Only a dim, rutted trail led to the place where the cabin overlooked a high bluff above the lake. Far below was the Omega Hotel, like a child's toy in the moonlight. The Indian explained that he had taken an opportunity to sneak Barney's car by devious back roads to this point.

The cabin was dark, and Danger struck a match and lit an oil lamp beside the front door before they went in. Blankets had been tacked up over the windows to keep the light from shining outside. The cabin consisted of only one room, fitted out with double bunks in a corner, an oil stove, and shelves of canned goods. Barney had forgotten his hunger and thirst. He pushed them aside again as he stared at the man sprawled on the lower bunk in the corner.

The man was Al Greeley. Barney recognized him from the photo he had found in Greeley's room in Jackson—big, dressed in sweat-stained khaki, with thinning dark hair and a heavy, puffy face, with a slack mouth and a flat brow. There was a long white scar on his right jaw that had not been in the photo Barney had seen. The scar stood out oddly against the deep tan on Greeley's face.

Blood had stained Greeley's right shoulder, and a crude bandage showed where the khaki shirt was torn away. The man was asleep or unconscious. His breathing made a harsh, irregular rasp in the quiet cabin, and there was a smell of sickness in the air.

"What happened to him?" Barney asked.

"I found him in the woods about two miles from Ferne's bungalow—where she was killed. He was drunk and wounded. I think one of Straehle's men may have spotted him and hit him with a lucky shot." Charley Danger looked down at the unconscious man with a dour expression. "He hasn't said anything sensible since I picked him up. He answers to his name, and that's about all."

"Maybe he needs a doctor."

Danger looked moody. "I took care of the bullet wound. I had some experience as a corpsman in Korea. It's not serious. The liquor in him is a lot more of a problem. I can't seem to dry him out."

"He hasn't told you anything?" Barney asked.

"He can't. He must have been on a bat for a week, with no food, nothing but cheap alcohol. Even if he comes to, he'll probably have the d.t.'s." Charley Danger's brooding eyes examined Barney with care. "You'd better sit down. I'll get you some coffee and food. Just a sandwich, but it ought to help."

Barney nodded and walked across the cabin to study the man in the bunk. There could be no sham about Greeley's condition. He felt for Greeley's pulse and found it fast and shallow. A fine, cool sweat beaded the man's brow, but he seemed to have no fever. Barney tasted the acid of frustration in him. Behind the debauched face of this man was the answer he wanted and needed, but it was locked away for hours to come, perhaps forever. Anger filled him.

Then a muttering came from the unconscious man. Barney bent over him and slapped his face quickly.

"Greeley! Come on, wake up."

"G'way. . ."

"Can you hear me?"

"Ma. . ." the big man said. "Mama. . ." His eyes were open, narrow and close-set, china blue and blank. "Sick . . . I'm sick. . ."

"Where've you been?"

"School. . . Sorry, mama. . . ."

The empty eyes closed and there was silence. Charley Danger was heating coffee on the kerosene stove and making a thick sandwich.

Barney moistened his dry mouth. "He's back in his childhood."

"That's all I could get out of him, too," Danger said. "But when I left you in Jackson, I scouted the bars where Greeley usually hangs out. I got some dope that may be interesting. You remember you wondered how the man who was with Mal Hunter up in Canada could have gotten back here in Omega?"

"It's been bothering me," Barney said, nodding.

"Al Greeley flew him back. I checked the Jackson Airport. He chartered a plane two days after Hunter disappeared and came back the next day. Alone both times, but that doesn't mean anything. It figures to make your theory pan out, Barney. Whoever flew up to Canada with Mal Hunter made an arrangement with Greeley to pick him up two days later. The Indian's dark eyes had small lights in them; his mouth was grim. "Of course, the man who hired Al could still be Malcolm Hunter."

"Maybe," Barney said. "But I doubt it."

Danger pointed to the cup.

"Drink your coffee."

"Al has the answer," Barney said. "He was paid off plenty. The landlady mentioned his having had a lot of money last week. He knew what had happened up in Canada, or he guessed, and he was being paid for silence. Then Ferne wheedled the answer out of him, got him drunk or boastful, and she knew the answer then, too.

And she started a bit of blackmail. Not such a little bit, either. She leaned on it too much and the murderer had to finish her off last night."

A snore came from the man sprawled on the bunk. Barney ate hungrily, drank a third cup of coffee. Except for a general stiffness from his bruises, he felt better and stronger. Yet fatigue clouded his efforts to think the matter out. Nervous tension would not permit him to rest. He could not sit and wait in stolid patience as Danger's temperament permitted. A sense of pressure, of events building to a climax, possessed him, together with an uneasy feeling of threat from every quarter. He was not worried for himself. But the action of the murderer in killing Ferne indicated a desperation to cover up guilt that could readily lead to other deaths. Somebody, Barney told himself, had to listen and accept what he knew, and act with authority on it. With the police after him, he felt helpless as if he were still in the hands of the two hoodlums.

He made his decision abruptly and stood up. The night outside was calm and clear. For a change, the woods were silent. Far below, the lake glistened in the moonlight, and beyond it the houses of Omega shone with many pinpoints of light. It was only ten o'clock.

"Have you got a gun?" Barney asked. "I'm going into Omega."

Danger's dark eyes were curious. "Now? The way you are?"

"There isn't any choice. I can't stay here. But you can watch Greeley and if he comes to, you can get the truth out of him. The trouble is, it might be too late by then. Someone else might die before you wring him out."

"You're taking a big chance. Straehle might pick you up. Why the gun?"

"To make sure I'm *not* picked up."

"You were a cop once, weren't you, in New York?"

Barney nodded. "Yes."

"You wouldn't shoot another cop, would you?"

Barney said: "I may not need the gun for shooting. Just for persuasion. I'm going to see Straehle."

"Are you crazy?" Danger snapped. "You can't do that."

"I've got to make somebody in Omega listen to me," Barney said. "I'll try to convince Straehle, first."

Charley took a Colt .38 from his back pocket and handed the automatic to Barney with a shrug. "Better clean up a bit before you go into town," he suggested quietly.

It was a shopping night in Omega, and most of the stores fronting on the courthouse square were brightly lighted and crowded with shoppers. Many of the summer people wore light toppers and sweaters over their vacation clothing, and their cars crowded the parking areas set aside for the stores. Barney drove slowly around the square and finally selected the railroad depot as the best place to leave his car. He did not know if the police were alerted to spot the coupe he had rented, and he left the door unlocked when he got out.

Only one or two curious glances were given by passers-by to his bruised and battered face as he walked back. Music blared from a juke box in a taproom, competing with the thumping rhythm of a recording from a record shop. Lights shone from the windows of Straehle's office, but the rest of the ornate limestone courthouse was in total darkness. The arched arcade that led inside was equally deserted. Iron stairways led up to interior galleries, and he mounted them swiftly, hoping the doors above were unlocked.

The doors were open. The marble corridor led him toward the lighted, frosted glass entrance to Straehle's office, and here he paused, his hand on the gun in his pocket. If Straehle was not alone, he would have to try something else. Listening, he heard the mutter of a man's voice, but there was no reply to the steady talking, and he assumed it came from dictation. He palmed the knob and let himself softly into the outer office, which was dark.

Through the opposite doorway he could see a portion of Straehle's desk under the light of a large gooseneck lamp, and one corner of the dictaphone machine. For a moment Straehle's voice muttered on, then abruptly broke off, and the D.A.'s high, sharp voice called: "Who is out there?"

Barney stepped through the doorway with the gun in his hand.

Straehle still wore his severe blue business suit, prim bowtie, and carefully squared white handkerchief in his breast pocket. His sharp face turned the color of suet as he stared at Barney's tall figure filling the entrance. His glasses glinted as his head jerked up.

"My God!" he whispered. "You!"

His hand darted for a button on his desk, then halted as Barney spoke briefly. "Don't. I'm here as a friend."

"Friend?" Straehle whispered. "Damn you, you've caused me more grief than anyone I've ever known! You must be insane!"

"Desperate, rather. Relax." Barney reached over and snapped off the dictaphone machine. "You're going to listen to me."

"Not for a minute!" Straehle's voice lifted, grew shrill, and then at a gesture of Barney's gun, quieted again. He said shakily: "You killed Ferne Kane. You killed her to cover up evidence."

"You're talking through your hat and you know it," Barney said. "There's nobody else here to listen to that nonsense except me, and you don't have to pretend right now. You must have checked my record back in

New York. You know I was a cop back there. And I had a damned good record."

"Until your wife died," Straehle snapped.

"That's right."

"You turned into a lush then," Straehle said, biting off his words with satisfaction. "You fouled up on an important case—the Ryerson matter."

"Yes. I admit I drank too much for a while. But that was a year ago. I've gone into practice of law for myself, since then. It's ancient history."

"Not to me. You're not a man to be trusted. Do you think you can intimidate me with your gun?" Straehle's face shone with sweat. Light from the desk lamp splintered off his glasses. His sharp nose looked white, and his tight purse of a mouth smiled grimly. "You wouldn't dare use that gun on me."

"Don't try anything," Barney said. "Don't tempt me."

"What do you want?" Straehle whispered.

"I want the truth, that's all. I want to know who tipped you about Ferne's murder and who told you I was there."

"It was a John Doe call."

"To you?"

"One of the desk sergeants at Hendrycks' headquarters took the message."

"Did the sergeant recognize the voice?"

"No," Straehle rasped. He leaned forward over his desk. "Do you quite realize what you are doing, Forbes? Mal Hunter knows you fooled around with his wife the other night. It's common gossip in town. And don't ask me how such word got around. It always does. When Mal Hunter catches up with you, he'll kill you."

"Can he commit murder in Omega and get away with it?"

Straehle sweated. He sat back a little, staring coldly at Barney. His pudgy hands made restless motions over

his desk blotter. "It would be your own fault," he muttered. "He could claim defense of his home. The un-
written law. It would be easy for him."

"You mean you would make it easy," Barney said. "But
I don't happen to be afraid of Malcolm Hunter. I seem
to be the only man in Omega who doesn't shake in his
boots when his name is mentioned. Maybe it's because
I'm the only one who is convinced that Malcolm Hunter
is dead."

"Then how do you account for his calls to Branthorpe,
who says he saw him yesterday—"

"Felix is lying."

"And his calls to Jase Franklyn?"

"I can't explain it—yet."

"You can't explain anything," Straehle sneered. "You
have no answers ready, yet you come in here with a gun
and expect me to listen to a lot of nonsense—"

"I expect you to listen to me," Barney said, cutting
him off. "I want to give you something to think about.
You've stood in the way of solving this case from the
very beginning, because of Mal Hunter. To you, Malcolm
Hunter is the end and the means of everything you hope
to get, everything you've staked your career on. You're an
ambitious man, they tell me. You have a fine political
future. And you think you need Malcolm Hunter to lift
you up to where you want to go. But all you actually
need is honesty and a little courage."

Straehle whispered: "I need Malcolm Hunter's help.
I've built my life on that fact."

"Hunter is dead," Barney said harshly. "You've been
playing politics and running away from a ghost."

There was silence in the office. From the street below
came the occasional sounds of traffic, muted voices, the
slam of a car door, a sudden blaring horn. Straehle said
nothing. He folded his hands on the desk before him
and stared at them. His nose was pinched, his mouth was

white. Barney waited, watching the struggle on the D.A.'s face. Straehle shook his head as if to clear it, started to speak, then was silent again. When he looked at last at Barney, his eyes were bleak, empty, and hard.

"I can't risk it," he said quietly. "You have no proof."

"If Malcolm Hunter is still alive," Barney told him, "then it must have occurred to you that he's really the one who killed Alex Kane and Ferne. Do you still plan to cover up for him, if that's the case?"

"I don't know."

"Meaning you will?"

"I can't say."

"But if he's dead," Barney went on, "you know that you've frustrated every honest effort to find the real killer. You know, deep inside yourself, that it isn't Charley Danger. And I'm not the man you want, either. You haven't looked anywhere else—you've been so busy running from Malcolm Hunter's shadow."

"Get out of here," Straehle whispered. "I've heard just about enough."

"I need your help," Barney said stubbornly.

"Get out!"

Barney stood up. He was defeated. He put his gun in his pocket, and as he did so, he felt the sunburst watch-fob he had picked up in Ferne Kane's bungalow. He took it out and dropped it on Straehle's desk. "Do you recognize this?"

Straehle poked at it with a stubby white finger, then lifted his head. His eyes glinted oddly. "Where did you find this?" he rasped.

"It was left for me to find, deliberately, near Ferne's body last night."

"It's Malcolm Hunter's," Straehle said.

"Yes. You can keep it for a souvenir."

Straehle did not seem to hear. He sat very still behind his big desk, looking at the bit of golden jewelry, but not seeing it at all. Barney went to the door and left the office without glancing back. There was no instant shout of alarm, no pursuit as he walked down the empty, echoing iron stairway to the interior courtyard and then mingled with the shopping crowd on the street. At the corner where the next street led to the railroad depot, he looked up at Straehle's lighted office windows.

As he watched, the lights abruptly went out.

20

HE FOUND Jake Hendrycks' house in the telephone book
and drove to the address ten minutes later. The house
was on a side road off the highway to the north, a former
farm home of gray shingles and a sagging picket fence
enclosing a lawn that had been beaten to exhaustion by
the children's play. Behind the house was a grove of
neglected fruit trees, a chicken shed, and a slanting barn
used as a garage. Barney stopped in the lane, and in the
light from the windows watched a white goat move
sleepily away from him. Two hound dogs slept on the
front porch, along with half a dozen cats. Everything
about the place was touched by decay and neglect.

Barney rang, tried to see through the curtains on the
front door, and rang again. The lights that were on in the
house were all in the rear. From the center of town came
the brazen sound of the courthouse bell, ringing eleven
times. The wind felt cool. He hammered on the door.

Footsteps tapped beyond the curtained door. It opened
and a slim woman whose faded hair and face might once
have been of unusual beauty stood there, looking at him.
She had dark hair streaked with gray and enormous,
tired black eyes, like ripe olives. She wore a cotton print
dress and a crisp apron over it.

"What is it?" she asked quietly.

"I want to see Jake Hendrycks. Is he in?"

She hesitated, searching his face.

152

"It's important," Barney said urgently. He told her his name. "Please tell him I'm here."

Her face lost some of its tired look. It could have been a happy face, but something had happened to it recently and she had forgotten how to smile. "Come in," she said. "But please be quiet. The children are in bed, except Violet and Joe. They've gone to the movies. Jake was telling me about you, Mr. Forbes."

"Where is he?"

"In the kitchen. He's sick."

Something suddenly crashed as she spoke, the sound coming from the back of the old farmhouse, as if a chair had been kicked over. Barney heard Hendrycks' muttered curses in the kitchen. He looked at the small woman, but he could read nothing in her sorrowing eyes. In silence, then, he followed her down a long hallway to the lighted room in the back of the house.

Hendrycks sat at the kitchen table, an empty bottle of bourbon on the floor beside him, another that was partially empty clutched between his big hands, resting on the table. His seamed and weathered face was stamped by an expression of drunken despair. He paused with the bottle lifted halfway to his lips and stared at Barney and whispered: "By God. By God, it's you. Franny, when did *he* show up?"

"Just now. I think he's foolish, but here he is."

"Get him a glass, Franny. He looks like he needs something. He ought to be drunk tonight, not me."

"Don't bother, please," Barney told the woman. "Why do you think I'm foolish to have come here?"

She shrugged and looked at her husband. The sorrow changed to pity in her dark olive eyes. "You said something to Jake that's been eating him all day and all night, ever since you said it. You said it to him last night, and he hasn't been the same since. You didn't trust him."

"Leave us alone, Franny," Hendrycks said harshly.

Shrugging, she went out, her shoulders straight, her feet making soft whispering sounds on the floor. Barney took a kitchen chair and reversed it and sat down with his arms folded across the back. Hendrycks picked up his glass with a shaking hand and drained it with two mighty swallows. He wore wide green suspenders over his sweaty khaki shirt, and his cartridge belt and holstered gun sagged against his hip. His broad buttocks pressed heavily into his chair as if he were weighted there. His yellow-white hair was disheveled.

"What are you doing here, son?" he whispered.

"I've come to you for help. I've just talked to Straehle. He wouldn't give me anything at all. On the other hand, he didn't yell for his bully boys when I walked out, so maybe I shook him up a little. But I don't know. I'd like to shake you up a bit, too, Jake. If I said anything wrong to you the other night, I'm sorry. I'm sorry I had to slug you, too. I wanted to find Ferne. I did, but I was too late. You believe that, don't you?"

Hendrycks looked down at his shaking hands. "I never begrudged your hitting me last night, son. I reckon I deserved it. And I reckon you can hit me again, because I got to give you the same answer Straehle just gave you. I can't help you."

"Is it still Malcolm Hunter?"

Hendrycks nodded, still looking down at his gnarled hands.

"Hunter is dead," Barney insisted harshly. "You're on the run, too, just like Straehle and everyone else in Omega. As you said, every man has his personal reasons. Straehle has his ambition, and you feel old and beaten and you're afraid that if you take a wrong step in this case, because it involves Mal Hunter, he'll have you out of your job and you'll go to the poorhouse."

"Yeah." It was a tired, exhausted word, dragged from the depths of the chief's big chest.

"You're running from a shadow," Barney told him. "There is no Malcolm Hunter. Hunter is dead."

"You're the only one who says so."

"It's the truth," Barney said.

"But nobody believes you. Not Straehle and not me, and not even Jase Franklyn."

"Is Jason afraid, too?"

Hendrycks frowned and sat even more heavily in his chair. His breathing was raw and gusty. "Funny thing. Jase took a bad licking from Mal Hunter and Mal swindled him out of that newspaper. It killed his mother, or so Jase says, and he always used to figure the sun rose and set by his ma. He was a broken man ever since. But he don't really seem to be afraid of all this like Straehle and me. Maybe it's because he figures he's already lost everything he ever wanted."

Barney said bluntly: "Jake, do you know who killed Alex and Ferne Kane?"

"No, I don't."

"You don't believe it was Charley Danger, do you?"

"I can't say, son. He has reasons—Charley, I mean. He could have done it. I like Charley, but he's a man of secrets, like a man who doesn't need anything or anybody in the world. I just don't know."

"Do you think Mal Hunter is in Omega?"

"He's here, all right."

"Then get your coat," Barney said roughly. "If Hunter is alive and if he's in Omega, let's go find him."

Hendrycks did not move. He looked up once at Barney and then his pale eyes swung quickly and shamefully away. He filled his glass and drank again. The second bottle was almost empty. Outside, one of the hounds began to howl and was almost immediately silent again. Barney looked up and saw Mrs. Hendrycks staring at her husband. Her face was remote and untouched, her eyes absorbing only the tragedy that lived in her man. Barney suddenly felt very tired.

"Jake," she said quietly. "Please go with him. You know that he's right. Go and find Hunter."

"Franny, let me alone."

"Go face him! If he's a killer, you've got to arrest him. He's no better than anybody else. And maybe a lot worse. Mr. Forbes is right. You can't keep running away and still live with yourself. You can't live here with me any more, if you do."

"Franny!"

The woman went on: "I don't care for myself, Jake. I know you're worried about me and the children. But some things are more important than bread. Or a roof over our heads. It's your honor, Jake. It's being a man. It's doing the job you always used to do. So I can be proud of you, as I've always been."

The big man suddenly drove the glass off the table with a wide sweep of his arm, and as the tumbler crashed to the floor he picked up the bottle and threw it against the wall. He lurched to his feet, his face white under the weathered tan. Neither Barney nor the woman moved. Abruptly, Hendrycks lurched to the back screen door and smashed it open and strode out of the house, into the dark night that brooded with the singing of insects in the orchard beyond.

Barney stood up slowly.

The woman said: "You can stay here tonight. You'll be safe. Jake won't turn you in." Her voice seemed to come from somewhere far away. "I'm sorry. I guess I've got to apologize for him."

"I'm sorry, too," Barney said. "Go easy with him."

"Yes. For the children."

Barney nodded and went out.

21

He found a public phone in a drugstore on the way back to town and looked for Malcolm Hunter's name in the directory; when he got it, he dialed the number. On the opposite side of the lake, the telephone rang and rang, four or five times, and there was no answer. He did not hang up. It was eleven-thirty. He thought of Evelyn and he thought of Lil and suddenly he realized he missed New York and wanted to be back there. His head ached. The phone kept ringing. There were other aches, deep inside his body, that reminded him of Chaz. Nobody wanted the case solved. Charley Danger, maybe. Nobody else. No one cared. There wasn't even a client left for him, if he judged Jan Hunter correctly. There was no reason why he should stay in Omega and get killed, and he knew this would happen, because somewhere in the town there was one who feared him, who thought he knew too much, when all he had were the loose ends of a tangled skein, leading nowhere, going nowhere. There was a shadow over the town, and they were all running away from it. He didn't want to run. He couldn't run. He wanted to find the shadow and see if there was any substance behind its menace.

The phone was still ringing.

He hung up.

It was a twenty-minute drive around the lake to the Hunter estate. He parked the car along the edge of the road, took a flashlight from the glove compartment, and

157

looked at the barred iron gateway to the English manor house. Then he walked away from it along the high stone wall until he came to its end in a mass of tangled brush. Circling it, he walked back along the inside of the wall to the edge of the lawn and then cut across the moonlit grounds to the silent house.

If there were servants, aside from the gateman and Felix Branthorpe, Barney saw no signs of them. No windows were alight. He circled one ivied wing, using the moonlight to guide his steps, and saw the shimmer of water in an oval swimming pool. He halted when he came to the terrace where he had first met Evelyn Hunter.

The French doors into the house stood open to the night breeze. There were rustlings in the yellow rose bushes and from across the lawn came the chirping of a solitary, chilly cricket. Turning, he studied the open doors that waited as if in invitation to him. There was only darkness beyond.

Using the flashlight, he probed the long sitting room, the dark oil paintings in massive frames on the wall, the shining brass of the fireplace equipment. There was nothing. No one. The house was silent. Quietly, then, he drifted to the main hallway, recalling the layout from his previous visit. No lights were visible. He had the feeling that the house was empty and deserted. But if so, where was Evelyn? And Felix? He went on, pausing at the foot of the sweeping stairway that led up to a paneled landing and the bedrooms beyond. A dim sound came down to him, remote and beyond definition. It was neither a voice, the wind, or music. Frowning, he snapped off the light and went up the stairs, guiding himself in the darkness by a hand on the smooth bannister.

Moonlight came through a tall curtained window at the end of the corridor, and he turned that way. The doors were closed on either side and he did not stop to investigate. Worry gnawed at him. The darkness and the silence in the big house seemed to hold an intangible presence that watched his searching progress with scorn and amusement. He took the gun from his pocket and held it ready and listened.

A whispering voice came to him. The faint sound of a man's deep laughter—a sound with no amusement in it, deep, harsh and unfamiliar.

It came from above, on the third floor.

Quickly, Barney returned to the stairs and climbed to the next level. These were the servants' quarters, he judged, when a quick squeeze on the flashlight disclosed cheaper carpeting and drably painted walls.

The laughter had changed to a low, metallic murmuring. It came from the right, and now he saw the dim glow of illumination from under a closed door at the far end of the corridor. Listening as intently as he could, he could make out nothing that was being said. There was an artificial quality to the sound that puzzled him, and then suddenly it became clearer and louder:

"Yes, this is Mal. Yes, that is . . . what I want you to do . . . I won't take no for an answer! Don't annoy me with your idiotic objections! Yes. . . ."

Barney pushed open the door and looked inside.

The room was small, fitted out as an office, with a gray steel desk and a small settee and gray filing cabinets set against the far wall. Simple dark draperies shielded the casement windows. The light came from a modern tubular lamp over the desk, where an elaborate tape recorder and splicing apparatus stood next to the telephone.

The door creaked slightly as Barney pushed it farther open, and there was a sudden swirl of movement inside the office.

"Hold it, Felix," Barney said quietly.

Felix Branthorpe stood frozen, staring at him. His hand hovered over the humming tape recorder.

"Don't touch it." Barney's words were sharp. "Move away from the desk."

"Where—where did you come from?"

"Never mind that. Your boys, Chaz and Henry, can explain how I got away from them—maybe. Where is Evelyn?"

"I don't know. She's gone."

"Where?"

"I don't know!" Branthorpe's voice lifted with an edge of unsuspected hysteria. He wore a dark turtle-necked sweater that emphasized his massive shoulders and depth of chest. Dark blue yachting sneakers squeaked a bit as he turned with his feet flat on the waxed floor. His tanned, handsome face regarded Barney with continued amazement. He attempted a blustering tone. "See here, you're trespassing, you know that? I don't know anything about Chaz and Henry. I've been here all evening, working on the estate accounts—"

"Splicing tape recordings of Malcolm Hunter's voice?"

Branthorpe looked venomous. His breathing rasped. "Put down the gun. I've been wondering how it would be to take you apart, ever since I first met you. Put down the gun, and we'll see."

"Shut up," Barney said. "Sit down."

"You can't—"

Barney hit him, driving the flat of the gun against his face. Branthorpe yelled in surprise and pain and fell backward, bleeding from the mouth. He hit the wall and lurched forward a step, fists doubled, then he halted. He sat down slowly and heavily. His face was blanched, his breathing was ragged. His eyes were dull.

"I didn't kill anyone," he whispered.

"What happened to Evelyn?"

"I don't know, I tell you!" Branthorpe cried. His eyes were fixed in fascination on Barney's gun. Then his glance swung to the tape recorder humming on the desk. He licked his lips, grimaced at the taste of blood in his mouth. "You can't prove anything. You haven't got anything on me."

Barney grinned. "I've got this tape. It tells a lot."

"They're only some old letters Mal Hunter dictated!"

"And which you have been snipping apart and splicing together to frame up telephone calls to Franklyn and Straehle and anyone else who needed convincing that Hunter was still alive!" Barney snapped. He felt a deep inner excitement, a quick moment of triumph. "Very neat, and why wouldn't it work?" he asked. "A voice on the telephone is much like any other voice that's electronically transcribed. Nobody would doubt it came from Mal, in the here and now. But it proves that you knew Malcolm Hunter was dead. You knew it all along. Yet you deliberately fostered the impression that he's still alive, here in Omega, by claiming to have seen him and by rigging phony calls from him with his taped voice!"

"It was a gag," Felix muttered. "Just a joke!"

"Murder is no joke. You wanted everyone to believe that Hunter was still alive, and you managed to convince them of it. I can see why you did it, too. Being estate manager, you didn't want to have any difficulty when you manipulated Malcolm's bank accounts. Knowing he's been dead for two weeks, you started siphoning off a lot of cash in the past two weeks, getting Evelyn to endorse your bank drafts and selling orders. How much have you socked away for yourself so far?"

Branthorpe sat still, his hands kneading his thighs. His face looked yellowish under the healthy summer tan. His eyes were sick. His mouth worked. "I—I don't know yet," he whispered. "I'm not sure."

"Were you working with Jan on this scheme?"

"No. He doesn't know about it."

"Or Evelyn?"

"No. It's all mine." Branthorpe looked up, his eyes gleaming with sudden hope. "There's plenty in it for both of us, you know," he said softly. "If you listen to reason, I'm willing to make a deal. I'll split with you. Nobody will ever be the wiser. You can be rich! You think I liked working for Mal Hunter? That sadistic son of a bitch is better off dead! The world is well rid of his kind! I haven't been greedy. What I've taken will never be missed. And it's covered perfectly. It would take an army of accountants to even begin to suspect that anything was wrong, and even then they could never trace it to me. It's safe. It's sure. You wouldn't have to worry about a thing, ever again. You could—"

"Shut up," Barney said. "You make me sick."

Felix wiped a hand across his mouth. His eyes were fever hot. He looked hungrily at the gun in Barney's hand, then looked at the tape recorder again. "Listen to me," he whispered. "You can't really prove anything against me, but I'm willing to go along with a deal just to save nuisance trouble for myself. Maybe Mal gave me the orders to fake those phone calls—did you think of that? Maybe that's what he told me to do before he left. Suppose I was just following orders?" His voice strengthened and grew harsh. "If you make trouble for me, I'll simply say that Mal knew he was in trouble with Alex Kane's death, and he had certain business matters and deals pending that might have suffered if it was thought he might be charged with a criminal offense. I'll say he told me to fake the phone calls to have people think he was back in Omega."

"You're lying," Barney rapped. "You know he's dead."

"No! I didn't say that!"

"But it's written all over you," Barney said. "In any case, your manipulations to milk the Hunter estate wouldn't stand an investigation at this present moment, would they?"

Branthorpe collapsed again. His breathing was heavy. "No. But in another day or two, it will be all right."

"So you know Mal Hunter is dead," Barney said quickly.

"Yes. Yes, I know it," Felix whispered. He seemed to shrink, to lose his size and vitality.

"Did you kill him?"

"No!"

"Did you kill Alex Kane?"

"No! I never killed anyone! I don't know who did it!" Branthorpe lurched up from his chair. His voice was shrill; his face glistened with sweat. "I swear I don't!"

"All right," Barney said. "I'll go along with it for a minute. But then we come to the big question, Felix. How did you know that Hunter was dead?"

Branthorpe was silent. He looked down at his hands. He looked quickly up at Barney, then away again. He moistened his brown lips.

"I won't tell you," he whispered.

"Then you'll tell it to the cops."

"If I tell you, it will all come out anyway. I know your kind. I got Straehle's report on you. They booted you off the New York police force last year. You made a heavy play for Evelyn the first chance you got when you came up here." Felix looked up with an angry sneer. "Think about my offer for a little while, and don't play so damned righteous with me. You'll buy it."

Barney hit him again. There was a deep, hot rage in him that pushed him to the very brink of his control. Felix fell to the floor, gasping, and held a hand to his face. There was a wild flame of hatred in his eyes.

Barney's voice was brittle. "You hired Chaz and Henry to take me out of the play, and I owe you plenty for that."

"You were beginning to get dangerous," Felix said

thickly. He took his hand from his face and stared mutely for a moment at the blood on his fingers. "They should have killed you."

"But they didn't. And they're probably running now. Chaz knows I'll kill him if I ever see him again. Meanwhile, I've got you on my hands, and you'll do even better, because they were only acting under your orders. Don't push me too far, Felix." Barney's voice shook. "I want answers. And I want them now."

Fear clouded the hatred in Branthorpe's eyes. "I don't know who killed Alex." He swallowed noisily. "I don't know what actually happened to Mal. I just know he's dead, that's all." He took a deep, shuddering breath. "It was Al Greeley who told me. He sold me the tip."

"When?"

"A week ago. Before you came here."

"And you believed him?"

"Why not? He—he told me he had gone up to Canada to pick up Mal at the lodge there. He—"

"On whose orders?"

"I assume Mal made the arrangements," Branthorpe said.

"You're lying again."

"I didn't ask Greeley! I was satisfied just with the proof he had!"

"And what was that?"

"He showed me a watchfob that Mal always carried with him. It was his good-luck piece. He was superstitious about it, and he never went anywhere without it. He'd never have parted with it unless it was stolen from him—or he was dead."

"And Al Greeley had it?"

"Yes."

"Did he give it to you?"

"Yes. As proof that Mal was dead."

"What did you do with it?"

"I lost it," Branthorpe muttered. "It's been worrying the life out of me. I don't know where or how I lost it, and if someone finds it and recognizes it, everybody will know that Mal must be dead."

"Somebody did find it," Barney said. "Somebody left it beside Ferne Kane's body."

Branthorpe swallowed again. His manner convinced Barney that he was telling the truth. It was quiet in the house except for the persistent humming of the tape recorder.

Branthorpe said quickly: "Al Greeley approached me for money. He said he could tell me the truth about Mal, and that I could make good use of the information. I didn't believe him or trust him, even after he showed me the watchfob. But I took a chance he wasn't lying. It worried me, that's why I— that's why I asked Chaz and Henry to question you about Mal. I still wasn't sure."

"Then you were still afraid Mal was alive?"

"It worried me, after I got started on the accounts. I had to know the truth." Branthorpe was sweating. "That's why I sent Chaz to find you. I swear I didn't know they'd get as rough as they did—"

"About Greeley," Barney said. "You paid him off?"

"I gave him a thousand dollars, cash, to keep his mouth shut."

"Then if it wasn't Greeley who flew up to Canada with Hunter that night, who was it?"

"I don't know," Felix said miserably. "I have no idea. I just took advantage of the situation to make something out of it for myself. I was sick to death of working for Hunter. I hated his guts. He never gave me anything without rubbing my nose in dirt first. He enjoyed humiliating me in front of other people. He'd insist on taking me with him to parties sometimes, and then he'd make a fool of me by ordering me around, telling me to do idiotic things. I had to keep on doing it. I needed the job. If

I'd quit, he'd have seen to it that I wouldn't get another job like this anywhere again. But I figured that some day my turn would come—and it did. When Jan telephoned, though, to say he was sending you up here, I got worried and hired those two hoodlums to keep an eye on you. That's all I had to do with whatever happened around here. I swear it."

The house was too silent, too empty.

"When did you last see Evelyn?" Barney demanded.

"She had dinner here. Then I sent away the cook and the man who gardens for us. I told them to take the weekend off, because I wanted the place to myself. I didn't want anybody listening to me while I tested the new batch of tape recordings I've been working on. Mal always insisted on recording all his telephone conversations. He said it saved a lot of argument on business affairs later, when he could play back exactly what he said. He also enjoyed taping the conversations he had with the women he played with. It just occurred to me to use them, that's all."

"When did Evelyn go out?" Barney persisted.

"About two hours ago. She took her own car."

"Did she speak to you when she left?"

Felix said dully: "She was upset because you and Charley Danger were missing. I don't know which of you bothered her the most. I never saw her like that before. I could usually handle her, but not this time. She was like a caged animal all day today—one minute walking up and down, up and down, and then just sitting and thinking and staring."

"What made her leave the house so suddenly?"

"She made a telephone call. I don't know who she spoke to. But I got the feeling that she was talking to another woman. You can usually tell by the tone of voice and expressions used. But she never mentioned the name. She was excited when she hung up. I jumped her about it—I wanted to know if she'd discovered anything that might affect me, because she looked so strange. I knew she was on to something. But I guess it didn't pan out, or she'd have been back with it by now."

"Maybe it did pan out," Barney said gratingly. "Maybe she walked right into something. Why didn't you follow her as you usually do?"

"I told you, I wanted to be alone to work on the tapes."

"You're sure she was speaking to a woman?"

"I think so." Felix felt a little more sure of himself. His wide, thin mouth smiled. "It probably didn't mean anything at all, you know. Evelyn thought she had something, the way I figured it at first, but since she was only talking to another woman, I didn't worry about it."

Barney stared at the chunky man without seeing him. The gun felt hot and slippery in his hand. Fear crawled in him—not for himself, but for the girl. Something slid elusively around in the back of his mind, but when he reached for it he could not find it. He almost had it. He paid no attention to Felix now. He was going back over the whole thing, remembering what had been said, by whom, and when. Nothing fitted, yet a pattern was there, indistinct and filmy, but nevertheless visible.

Felix said curiously: "You sound as if you think Evelyn is in trouble."

"I'm sure of it. She discovered who the murderer is."

"But how could she? She wasn't out of the house all day. She just sat around, hour after hour—"

"She remembered something—something that made sense. It added up to the answer for her. It's something she knows, and something I know, too." Barney stared at the man. "It lets you out. You can call yourself lucky."

The answer, Barney suddenly knew, was not in what people had told him so much, nor in what he had seen with his own eyes. It was more subtle than that. It was under the surface, in shades of meaning he had previously missed or overlooked, in attitudes, in fears and lack of fears, in the scorn in Ferne Kane's voice before she died. . . .

He shook his head angrily. His fear for Evelyn deviled his thoughts. She had gone deliberately into dark and dreadful danger. For himself, or for Charley Danger. She had not come back. She was dead. And with that thought came the desperate, sickening conviction that he had failed. First Lil, now Evelyn. But Lil's death had happened long ago, and nothing on earth could have prevented it and no one could have foreseen it. Here and now, if he had been quicker on his feet, smarter than he'd been, he could have saved Evelyn. The burden of his guilt doubled and trebled. It paralyzed him for several long, black moments.

Felix seized his opportunity. He jumped like a great cat for the door, slid through it, and was gone. His footsteps clattered with crazy speed on the stairs going down to the lower levels of the house. Barney snapped to his feet, ran after him to the head of the stairs, then halted in the darkness. He listened to Branthorpe's heels striking the terazzo floor of the big foyer below. A door slammed, raising strange echoes. Barney leaned against the bannister and started down slowly, not in pursuit, not going anywhere, his mind filled with the thought of Lil and Evelyn, the two girls strangely blended into one.

Light filtered through the tall stained-glass windows over the terrace entrance, filling the entrance hall with strange hues. It came to him abruptly, while he walked toward the massive front door.

He halted.

He stood very still while the pattern blossomed and unfolded in his mind like an evil flower.

It might not be too late.

Suddenly he began to run.

22

It was after midnight when he stopped the car in Kay Franklyn's driveway on the other side of the lake. The garage doors were open, and his headlights shone on the vacant interior. The prim little bungalow was in darkness. Barney made no effort to be silent. He let the car door slam as he got out and walked up on the porch and hit the front door with his fist. His knock went echoing emptily through the spinster's house. No one came to the door; no one called out to him. He went around to the back then, stepped up onto the kitchen stoop, and tried the rear door. It was kept shut only by a hook. He fumbled in his pocket for something to snap it up, found nothing, and started to wrench the door open by main force when it was suddenly opened to him and a large, bearish figure bulked before him in the inner darkness.

"No use destroying property, son. Walk right in."

It was Jake Hendrycks. Barney tasted sudden fear because of the cop's presence. Hendrycks stood like a massive monolith in the darkness of the kitchen, a gun in one hand, a flashlight in the other. There was something different in his manner and his bearing. In the dim light of the stars outside, his face looked graven of stone, his white hair and tanned features standing in curious contrast.

"Get out of my way," Barney said savagely. "I'm looking for Kay Franklyn."

169

"She isn't here, son."

"Have you seen Evelyn Hunter?"

"Nobody is here. I've been sitting and thinking alone in this place for an hour. Where have you been, Barney?"

"In and out of trouble." Barney stared at the big, shambling man. "What happened to you?"

"I sobered up. I thought about what you said to me. I did a lot of thinking and I took a long, good look at myself, son. I owe you something I can't ever repay."

"Still afraid of Mal Hunter?"

"Sure," Hendrycks said softly. He smiled. "But that won't stop me now."

"Hunter is dead," Barney said. "I've told you that, over and over again." Quickly, in the silent, shining little kitchen, he told the chief about Felix Branthorpe and the spliced tape recordings. Jake Hendrycks did not interrupt. His head came thrusting forward on his meaty shoulders and he listened with no change of expression on his slab of a face. Barney said: "The trouble is that Evelyn figured out something tonight and went to meet the murderer. She talked on the telephone to a woman, and the only other woman in this thing is Kay Franklyn. I'm sure of that much. I only hope I'm not too late."

"And you thought she was here?"

"Where else can she be?"

"Take it easy, son. You look a mite wild."

"I can't let her get killed," Barney said tightly. "Or hurt in any way. It's important to me."

"Are you in love with her?" Hendrycks asked gently.

"I don't know. I don't think so. It doesn't have anything to do with it. But I've got to find her before something happens to her, or I'll never forgive myself."

"You won't find her here," Hendrycks said bluntly. "I think we'd better go look somewhere else."

Barney stared at him. "Are you with me now?"

"All the way," Hendrycks said. "I ain't going home

until I can face my wife like an honest man."

"What are you doing here?"

"I think I figured out the same thing you did, Barney. It's an ugly thing. It fits only one party. But there's no proof, is there?"

"No," Barney said. "If Al Greeley talks, we'll have it. But I can't wait for that."

"I reckon not." Hendrycks drew in a heavy breath. "Come along. I'll help you."

Crickets chirped and katydids sang in the cool mountain night. Barney walked silently along a narrow path that threaded a patch of swamp. Hendrycks was just ahead of him, as silent as a huge cat, leading the way. The little swamp was like an oasis in the center of Omega, wild and untouched, though they could hear the muted sounds of traffic on the main street beyond the loom of nearby buildings.

Hendrycks halted at the edge of the swamp. The Victorian house of Jason Franklyn bulked just ahead, beyond the weedy, scrubby lawn. A light shone deep within the lower floor, and another, dimly visible, was glimpsed from behind drawn shades in one of the turreted cupola rooms high above. Hendrycks shook his head.

"All you've got is a hunch and a hope," he whispered. "But I hope you're right, Barney."

"Maybe we're not too late."

They drifted soundlessly up to a back porch. The door was locked. Hendrycks drifted like a shadow, amazingly silent for his size and weight, and indicated a tall, dusty window nearby. It slid up with only a slight squealing sound. They waited for a moment, but no one challenged them.

"Breaking and entering," Hendrycks said. "Jase won't like it. He'll never forgive me."

"Go around to the front door," Barney suggested. "I'll get inside this way. Give me a few minutes—make it five. Then come in as if you're making a friendly call."

Hendrycks seemed relieved. "Will you be all right?"

"We'll see," Barney said.

He waited until the big cop had vanished around a corner of the house before climbing inside over the high window sill. He left the window open behind him. He judged he was in a pantry room, and he crossed it quietly, pushing open a swinging door with his finger-tips. Light gleamed through a doorway opposite, as yellow as butter. He went that way, paused, listened, and went on. He was sweating. He stood in the dusty corridor that faced the front doorway. Beyond the stairs, the bronze statue of Mercury held aloft his yellow light bulb. Nobody was in sight. There was a smell of mildew and mice and dust in the still, silent air. A feeling of decay and disuse that went beyond mere neglect. The house was a monument, a mausoleum to honor a dead past that Franklyn refused to relinquish.

He found Kay Franklyn in the octagonal library he had visited before.

An antique lamp of milk glass shed a wan light over the gray-haired woman. She sat in a wing chair near the fireplace, alone and silent, unmoving. If she saw him enter, she gave no sign of it. She stared blankly into space. Only the quiet lift and fall of her spinster's bosom showed that she was alive. Her gray hair was neatly parted in the center and fixed in a prim bun at the nape of her neck. As always, her gray business suit was tidy and freshly pressed. She wore low-heeled oxford walking shoes, and there was thick mud on the soles.

"Miss Franklyn," Barney said quietly.

She looked at him, moving only her eyes. She spoke in a flat voice that was not recognizable as her own. "I knew you would come here. I told him you would come, sooner or later. I've been waiting."

"Where is Jason?"

"Gone."

"Where?"

"I don't know."

"Miss Franklyn, you know where he is," Barney said insistently. "You know how important it is that I see him tonight—as soon as possible. Before something else happens."

She moved her head slightly, tilting it as if listening for something. The cords stood out in her neck. Barney listened, too. He heard nothing. He smelled the dust and the decay in the house.

"Don't you want to help him?" he asked.

She said quietly: "I've tried."

"It's not too late."

"Oh, but it is."

He said: "Was Mrs. Hunter here?"

"Evelyn? Yes. She was here."

"Where is she now?"

"I don't know."

"She telephoned to you about something, didn't she?" Barney waited. For a moment he thought his words were lost in some gray fog that surrounded her. When at last she nodded, he said: "Miss Franklyn, do you want her to die?"

"It will be her own fault." She looked up at Barney with eyes that were suddenly and shockingly liquid with tears. Her mouth shook for a moment, then pressed into a thin line. "You understand, don't you?"

"No," he said harshly. "I'll never understand murder. She doesn't have to be killed."

"She called Jason tonight. She told him what she knew. That is, she knew it, but she didn't believe it, and he told

her to come here and they would see what could be
done."

"And then?"

The woman was silent. Barney felt a fear grow inside
him that could not be denied, rising like a foetid mist.
"Please," he said gently. "You can help me. She doesn't
have to die."

"It is too late."

"What did she suddenly learn?"

"It was something she always knew, it seems. It just
happened that she remembered what she had forgotten
or overlooked. She came here thinking that you or
Charles Danger might be here. I think Jason told her
something to that effect. She wanted to make a bargain
for your life. Or Charles' life. I'm not sure."

"She's not in love with me," Barney said. "It's Charles
she wants."

"Perhaps."

"And you love Jason, don't you?"

"I have always loved him."

"You've done everything you could for him, haven't
you?"

"Yes."

"You lied for him," Barney said.

"Yes."

"Did you know about Ferne?"

"It was insanity," she sighed.

"But nothing too unusual," Barney said. "It happens to
many men like that—quite often, at Jason's age. Ferne
knew all there is to know about men. She was not like
you. She was experienced. How could you have hoped
to compete with her? You never really stood a chance."

She stared at him. There were traces of silent tears
that had coursed down her face. "Then you know about
that, too?"

"I'm guessing," Barney admitted. "But it's the only thing that makes sense."

The woman's shoulders sagged. Her whisper was distant and given with an effort. "I couldn't fight her, you know. She was like some evil spell cast over him. She haunted his dreams. She laughed at him and taunted him and challenged him to do things for her that he would never normally have dreamed of doing. She possessed him completely. He was not sane."

"He's not sane now," Barney said. He was sweating again. There was no sign of Hendrycks at the front door. Where was he? Five minutes had long gone by. He listened to the silence in the house that was not a silence, but the whispering of ghosts long dead and forgotten. "Tell me where he is," he urged quietly. "You owe him no more loyalty. Where did he take Evelyn?"

"I owe him everything," the woman whispered.

"Why? Because he ignored you? Because he never so much as looked at you or thanked you for all the countless little things you constantly did for him?"

"I did not do it for thanks."

"Then you did it to help him. Are you helping him now, by letting him go through with this tonight?"

"I don't know," she whispered. She rocked silently from side to side for a moment. "I just don't know."

"Weren't you jealous of Ferne?" he asked abruptly.

"Oh, yes. Yes, of course."

"You hated her, didn't you?"

"Yes. With all my soul. I hated her."

"Did you kill her?"

She looked at him with opaque eyes. She drew a deep breath. "Yes. Yes, I killed her."

"You're lying," Barney said.

"No!"

Barney said: "Jason killed her. Jason killed Alex Kane, too. And Jason killed Malcolm Hunter."

"No! No!"

A voice spoke quietly from the doorway at Barney's back, cutting through the woman's shrill, sudden cry.

"Never mind, my dear. It is obvious that he knows."

Barney turned slowly.

It was Jason Franklyn.

23

FRANKLYN stood quietly in the doorway, slim and erect, his scholarly face etched with deep shadows. He wore the same odd Turkish slippers, the same velvet smoking jacket. His sensitive hands were plunged deep into the pockets of the jacket. He smiled. The twitch of his mouth was meaningless. He took a short step into the room and said:

"Jake Hendrycks will not be coming in, Barney. I left him on the porch. You need not be alarmed. He will be all right. Please drop your gun."

Barney stared at him. "Are you armed?"

"In my pocket," Jason said. "Please."

Barney dropped his gun. It made a small thud on the faded oriental carpet, bounced, and touched one of Miss Franklyn's muddied shoes. She made a muted noise in her throat and did not move. She stared at Jason. He smiled again.

"I am sorry, Katherine. Truly sorry."

"Are you?" she whispered doubtfully.

"There seems to be no end to it. None at all. It goes on and on. I have no liking or taste for it. It was meant to be simple and neat and very, very clean. An act of justice, an act of vengeance. But it did not end there." Franklyn stared broodingly at Barney. "It would have been better if you had never interfered."

"Where is Jan Hunter?" Barney asked abruptly.

"He is with Straehle. Jan is rather talkative about his

177

personal problems, and I took the opportunity to relay some of them to the district attorney. At the moment, Jan is answering a number of embarrassing questions about Ferne's visit to New York, some months ago. A side lane down which Straehle will travel without much speed but considerable effort."

"And Evelyn?"

"I am sorry."

"What have you done with her?"

"Suppose I told you that she is dead?" Franklyn smiled.

Barney trembled inwardly. Another small sound was choked off in Kay's throat. He looked sidewise at her. She sat as a bird might perch, on the very edge of her chair, her back ramrod straight, staring at Franklyn as if she had never seen him before.

"What did she guess about you?" Barney rasped.

"She saw me enter the plane with Malcolm, that night. She did not recognize me. She gave it no real thought until you disappeared yesterday, following Charley Danger's jailbreak. Apparently the pressure of her fears made her recall something about the figure she saw entering the plane that night—some mannerism, perhaps, that convinced her that it was I who flew to Canada with Malcolm." Franklyn shrugged his narrow shoulders. "And she was correct. Unfortunately for her. I bear her no ill-will. She thought you and Danger might be here, and I did not disillusion her when she advised me she was coming. I think she imagined she might strike a bargain with me, for your safety." Franklyn frowned. "But how did you come to learn about me?"

"May I sit down?" Barney asked. "I'm very tired."

"You do look ill, at that. Branthorpe's hoodlums apparently did desperate things to you." Franklyn's smile was again a quick, meaningless quirk of his lips. "Please remain standing, however. And answer my question. It is not idle curiosity. If you managed to guess the answer, others may follow the same path. After all, I must protect myself."

"It was nothing very specific," Barney said. "A number of little things. The main pattern was clear enough, once I went up to Canada. Somebody took advantage of Mal Hunter's quarrel with Alex Kane to kill Alex and frame Hunter for it, with only a minor side diversion created by dumping the body in the lake in front of Charley Danger's house. Alex was lured to the place where he was killed without ever knowing why. You had no reason to hate Alex, did you?"

"He was a simple young man. Often pleasant, as a matter of fact. But he was Ferne's husband. Ferne and I—" Franklyn waved a small white hand. "But you must know about that."

"Then you killed Alex for two reasons. One was to get rid of him as Ferne's husband, and the other, much more important, was to frame Malcolm Hunter. You never lost your hatred for Mal. You admitted it to me the first time we met. Probably you witnessed Mal's fight with Alex and saw an immediate chance to capitalize on it in several ways. Mainly, by revenging yourself on Mal for stealing the newspaper from you, and for all the subsequent petty humiliations you suffered at his hands. You considered him an unlettered brute, cruel and predatory and callous. You had plenty of time in the course of that night to make your arrangements with Al Greeley to fly up to Canada after you. Then you went to Hunter's house and told him that Alex was dead of injuries dealt him by Hunter's fists. You managed to panic Hunter into flight. You posed as his friend. He saw no harm in vanishing for a few days until the matter was cleared up and he organized his defenses. He certainly had no fear of you."

Franklyn spoke like a spiteful woman. "He held me in contempt. He laughed at me. He said he only kept me on as editor of the paper because I amused him. He didn't want to go that night. You're wrong about my persuasive powers. I had to force him to go with a gun in his back. He did the flying. Once he threatened to deliberately crash us, but I pointed out to him that life was far more precious to him than it was to me."

"And when you landed up there, you killed him."

"Certainly. And scuttled the plane. Accident, see?"

"And then Al Greeley picked you up and brought you back here. Kay covered up for your absence. You could count on her help. She said you were locked up in here working on your historical research. She loves you and she was willing to do anything for you."

The woman spoke in a flat voice. "No more, Jason."

"No more will be necessary, my dear," said Franklyn.

Barney paused, listening. There was no sound from outside. He wondered about Hendrycks. He could expect no help from that quarter, apparently, if Jason Franklyn was telling the truth. He went on:

"You had trouble with Al Greeley from the start, didn't you? When you hired him, you paid him well, enough to certainly guarantee his immediate silence until you made other plans for him. But you didn't know that he, too, was one of Ferne's many male friends. Ferne got the truth from Greeley right after I first met her—and set out to milk you of everything you owned. But you were still infatuated with her. She held you in contempt, but you were willing to give her anything she demanded. Where did she finally go over the line?"

Franklyn's face moved oddly in the wan light of the milk-glass lamp. "She laughed at me. She always laughed. I suppose I was clumsy, with no experience, really. I asked her to marry me. She said many spiteful, embarrassing things. And then she insisted that I give her the deed to this house. To my mother's house." Franklyn's voice lifted. "I had planned it quickly, but well, I

thought. I had stolen Alex's crossbow and used it because
Mal Hunter was well-known to be an expert archer. I
practiced archery quite often myself, back in the swamp
behind the house. No one knew about it. I don't know
why I never mentioned it—it seemed like a child's form
of amusement, then. But I was adept enough with the
weapon. I left it in your hand, to muddy the waters, of
course." He paused, brought back his thoughts to the
dead girl. "When Ferne asked me for this house, I saw
her true self at last. I saw there could never be any peace
for me as long as she lived. I could not have her, she
would never belong to me, and when the time came
when I had given her everything, I knew she would leave
me. I saw it all very clearly. I had thought at first that
getting revenge on Hunter would be enough; then I
wanted Ferne, too; and then I knew I had to be satisfied
with only the first goal. When I followed you to her
bungalow, I thought then that you knew the truth, too.
I tried to frighten you off, so you wouldn't find her and
speak to her. And then I had to knock you out. While
you were unconscious, Ferne scorned and mocked me.
I—I could stand it no longer. I had to show I was strong
enough—strong enough to kill her, too."

Barney said: "You knew Felix was deliberately creat-
ing the illusion that Hunter was still alive?"

Franklyn nodded quickly. "It naturally suited my
purpose. I was willing to help him. I did not care what
he stole from the Hunter estate. I never wanted money.
I planted the fob to indicate that maybe a live Mal had
killed Ferne. Greeley had stolen it from me and sold it
to Branthorpe, but I stole it back."

"You should have gone through with one more killing,"
Barney said. "Doing away with Evelyn and me won't
help you now. Greeley told Felix Branthorpe the truth.
Felix knows it now. And Greeley will tell others. That's
the kind of man you chose to trust. You're rather pitiful,

Jason, with your lack of knowledge of the world and women. You've lived in the past so much, with idealized images of yesterday's heroic figures, that you forget what real flesh-and-blood people are often like today."

"Did Greeley tell you about me?" Franklyn whispered.

"It wasn't necessary. Everyone was afraid of Hunter. They all ran away from his shadow. All except you. Somehow, although you admitted hatred of him, you never showed fear. You encouraged fear in Jan Hunter, but there was none in you. When I was suddenly struck by that realization tonight, I knew that you, too, knew that Hunter was dead. And you had to be the man who flew up to Canada with him and killed him there."

Barney halted, then went on: "And there was another thing. I wasn't completely knocked out up there in Ferne's bungalow, before you killed her. I heard you quarreling with her. I heard you on your knees, pleading with her. And I heard the way she spoke to you. Ferne knew how to handle men. She feared most men, underneath her hard shell of tough sophistication. She would never have dared to express her contempt for any other man involved in this affair—except to someone like you. Because she thought she could control you. Because she had you on your knees. And since she hated men, she despised you once she got you there. When I remembered the sound of her voice and yours, I knew it was you who killed Ferne—and all the rest of it fell into place."

"Where is Greeley now?" Franklyn asked. His voice was high, strangely womanish, with an undertone of sharp hysteria. His face was white. "Where is he?"

"With Charley Danger."

"Where?"

Barney shook his head. "You'd better give me your gun and take me to Evelyn," he said quietly. "You certainly are smart enough to see you can't win any more."

"Where is Greeley?" Franklyn asked. His voice was close to a shout. He took his hand from the pocket of his smoking jacket and pointed the gun he held at Barney. "I want to know."

"Jason—" Kay began.

"Stay out of this, Kay."

"Jason, please!"

"Damn you for a simpering old woman!" Jason shouted. His face was suddenly flushed, his eyes wild. "I'm sick and tired of having you whimpering around me, always touching me, always asking what you can do for me! Do you think you can take Mother's place with me? Do you think I need you or want you?" His voice rose to a shriek. "Get out of my sight! Go unstairs and see that everything is all right up there. But leave me alone! Do you understand?"

Kay Franklyn stood up, very slowly. She had changed. She had been a trim, middle-aged business woman a moment ago. Now she had aged. Her face was blanched. Her eyes were deep dark holes against the bone-white of her skin. She spoke in a deep, ugly whisper.

"Jason, I never, never dreamed that I offended you. I only wanted to help. Even when you lost your head like a schoolboy over that young tramp, I understood. Or I thought I understood. I told myself that you were too fine, too grand and too clever, to be seriously misled by that girl. When you got into trouble over her, I helped you. Now you have no right to speak to me like this."

"Get out!" Jason shrieked. "Get out, you old bitch!"

She stooped quietly and picked up the gun. Jason paused with his mouth open, staring at her.

The gun crashed before Barney could move. The explosion was thunderous inside the room. Barney did not know if the shot went home or not as Jason whirled, stumbled, and plunged from the library. There came a grunting sound from the hallway, and a thud. Barney

ran for the door. Chief Hendrycks stood there, bulking
in huge anger. Jason sat slumped against the wall, staring
with unbelieving eyes at the stain of blood that oozed
from his chest.

Hendrycks lifted his big head, looked at Barney.

"You shot him?"

"Kay did it."

"Get her gun."

Barney went back into the room. Kay Franklyn sat in
the wing chair beside the cold fireplace. Her face was
the color of ashes. The gun lay in her lap, and she did
not resist him or lift her head to look at him when he
picked it up.

"Stay here," Barney said. "Where is Evelyn?"

"Upstairs," she whispered. "In his mother's room."

Barney swung out of the room with a long step. Hendrycks was examining Franklyn. He took the stairs two
and three at a time, swung on the newel post at the landing, and went on up to where he had seen a light in the
turret cupola from outside. The door was not locked. He
paused on the threshold, feeling a squeeze of apprehension in him.

It was a bedroom, like something out of a museum
with its ornate brocaded draperies, the massively carved
bed and lace tester, the marble-topped dressers with
shining, waxed walnut drawers. There was an incredible
hodge-podge of bric-a-brac, but unlike the rest of the
house, this room was cared for, dusted, cleaned and
waxed. A pink-fringed lamp shone on the giant tester
bed. Evelyn was there, bound hand and foot, gagged.

Barney felt dry relief in his throat as her eyes swung
to him with a flash of white. He saw her quick hope as
she recognized him. He went toward her slowly, smiling.

24

THE HEAT of the sun pressed down on him like a warm, comforting hand. He lay face down, flat on his stomach on the gently rocking float, listening to the sounds of the lake, the dim racketing of an outboard motor, the high shouts of distant water skiers. It was two days later. He had spent one day in the local hospital, sleeping the clock around. Most of the next day had been spent with Straehle and Jan Hunter.

Franklyn was dead. No charges had as yet been pressed against Katherine Franklyn. Probably none would ever be made. He did not want to think about it. He was content with this physical relaxation, soaking in the healing warmth of the sun, feeling the lake breeze on his shoulders and back.

Jake Hendrycks shared the float with him. The chief wore his usual khaki uniform, stained with sweat under the armpits, his cartridge belt and gun sagging against one broad hip. The lake breeze stirred his thick white hair. He had been talking quietly about Omega, but Barney had not truly been listening. Behind them, secure on the high pillars that lifted it above the slope of the mountainside, was Charley Danger's house. He felt a serenity and a peace of mind he had long forgotten.

"About those two hoodlums," Hendrycks said, and his voice indicated he was repeating himself. "What do you want done with them?"

"Where did you say you picked them up?"

"The state cops got 'em about twenty miles south of Omega. Cracked up in the car they stole. The little fat one, Chaz, says he's happy to be in jail. Says you can't get at him as long as he's behind bars." Hendrycks grinned. "You want to press charges?"

"None of a personal nature."

"You don't hate for very long, do you, son?"

"No," Barney said.

Hendrycks sighed. "Well, we'll put 'em away for concealing evidence, and for conspiring toward criminal extortion and embezzlement. Same charges we got Felix on. Straehle will have a ball with it."

"Is Felix out on bail?"

"Not yet. It's fixed at twenty thousand. Impeding the progress of the law, concealing evidence of homicide, and so forth. . . . You mind if we walk back into the shade and have a beer?"

"I like the sun," Barney said.

"I'm too old for it. . . . You were bluffing that night at Franklyn's, weren't you?"

"Not so much a bluff," Barney said. "I just had no real proof. But he convicted himself when he turned Kay against him."

"I feel real sorry for that little woman."

"She was in love with him," Barney said. "People do things like that. She never really saw him the way he was. What about Al Greeley?"

"His confession is signed and sealed and in Straehle's safe. No trouble there, once we got him dried out. He talked easy, that man. He was scared."

"And Charley Danger?"

"He ought to be here any minute," Hendrycks said. "How long are you going to fry out here?"

"Until train time," Barney said.

"You're leaving Omega?"

"Back to New York. Back to the job."

"This outfit of lawyers you work for—you'd like that better than a job with me in Omega?"

"I don't want to stay here," Barney said. "I don't think I should."

He did not elaborate any further. A car came down the lane and Charley Danger and Evelyn got out of it and came walking down to the lake front and the float. Barney watched the girl. She had a free, swinging walk, like Lil; her dark hair shining in the sun had secret red highlights, like Lil's; and she looked at Charley in the same way that Lil had always looked at him.

He knew he had to leave Omega.

Charley waved and said something to Evelyn and strode into the house, calling out something about beer. Hendrycks sighed and got heavily to his feet, rocking the float. His eyes swung from Barney to the approaching girl.

"I think I see what you mean, Barney. I'll be moseying along into the shade. It's the only place for a duffer like me. You want a lift to the depot?"

"I'll accept the invitation this time," Barney grinned.

"Then I'll be back."

He was gone, and Evelyn settled gracefully in his place on the float. There were flecks of gold in her eyes. She wore a white linen dress with a wide red cinch belt that enhanced the soft flair of her hips. Her perfume touched him and he sat up, aware of the loose fit of Charley Danger's old khaki trunks that he had borrowed.

"Barney, this is the first and only chance I've had to properly thank you . . . for everything," she began quietly.

"You don't owe me anything," he told her. "I was doing a job. I'll get paid for it."

"You're bluffing. We haven't much time alone like this —Charley will be along soon. Please be honest with me, Barney. I—I'm a little confused."

"About what?"

"You—and Charley."

"Can't make up your mind?"

"It isn't that. I—"

"It's Charley for you, isn't it?"

"Yes," she said, nodding. Her dark hair shone smoothly in the sunlight. Her lips were moist and parted. Her eyes were grave as she studied him. "Have you told Charley —about that night here?"

He met her gaze levelly. "What is there to tell?"

She bit her lip. "You weren't in love with me then—and you're not now, are you?"

"No."

She seemed relieved. "It was your wife you were thinking of?"

"Yes. I was thinking of Lil."

"Is it all right now?"

"Yes," he said.

She looked at him searchingly and then seemed to straighten with an inner relief. She exhaled softly. "I'm so glad—so glad it's better for you. And—I do thank you, Barney. I love Charley. I've always loved him, from the first moment we met. But we never—we couldn't even speak about it. We didn't dare, while Mal was—" She checked herself, touched his hand, rested her fingers on his. "Will you stay in Omega for a while?"

"I'm leaving tonight. I think it's better."

She leaned toward him and kissed him. It was just a kiss. "Thank you. I'll never forget you."

There came a hail from the house and they saw Charley Danger walking down toward the float with a tray containing several cans of beer. Barney looked at Evelyn as she watched the other man approach. Her eyes shone, and there was a softness to her mouth, in her whole body that seemed to lean toward the man coming toward them.

Barney looked away at the shining blue lake, the lift of the mountains, dark green under the late summer sun. The sun pressed warm hands on his shoulders. A squirrel ran up a tall pine, chattered at him for a moment, then vanished with a flick of its bushy tail. He remembered what Jason Franklyn had said about Omega being the world, and all the world being encompassed in Omega. Everything a man wanted could be found right here. But he had not found it. And this did not trouble him and he knew it would not trouble him any more in the future. It was all right about Lil, at last. Evelyn had made it all right. He had come, not to the end of a long, dark road, but to a turning.

He sat there after Evelyn got up to meet Charley, and he looked at the peaceful sunlight on the lake for a long, quiet time.

THE END